SAMATYA

*An Egyptian Woman Among
the Children of Israel*

MOHAMED ADLY

Published by

MELROSE BOOKS

An Imprint of Melrose Press Limited
St Thomas Place, Ely
Cambridgeshire
CB7 4GG, UK
www.melrosebooks.co.uk

FIRST EDITION

Copyright © Mohamed Adly 2017

The Author asserts his moral right to
be identified as the author of this work

Cover by Melrose Books

**ISBN 978-1-912026-26-5
epub 978-1-912026-27-2
mobi 978-1-912026-28-9**

All rights reserved. No part of this publication may be reproduced, stored in a retrieval system, or transmitted, in any form or by any means electronic, mechanical, photocopying, recording or otherwise, without the prior permission of the publishers.

This book is sold subject to the condition that it shall not, by way of trade or otherwise, be lent, re-sold, hired out or otherwise circulated without the publisher's prior consent in any form of binding or cover other than that in which it is published and without a similar condition including this condition being imposed on the subsequent purchaser.

Printed and bound in Great Britain by:
CMP (UK) Ltd, G3 The Fulcrum, Vantage Way
Poole, Dorset, BH12 4NU

Dedication

Praise be to God. I dedicate my first book to my mother and father, to whom I owe my life, and am grateful to them both.

Mohamed Adly

Contents

Foreword		vii
Chapter I	An Evening on the River Nile	1
Chapter II	Inside the Pharaoh's Palace	8
Chapter III	Hori's Dreams	12
Chapter IV	A Hard Night	15
Chapter V	Malissa and Samatya	23
Chapter VI	In the South	32
Chapter VII	Among the Children of Israel	35
Chapter VIII	Rachel and Samatya	39
Chapter IX	Aborted Dreams	46
Chapter X	The New House	54
Chapter XI	The City Market	61
Chapter XII	Preparation for the Festival	70
Chapter XIII	News from the Royal Palace	74
Chapter XIV	The Buds of the Garden	79
Chapter XV	The Festival Day	84
Chapter XVI	The Three Friends	98
Chapter XVII	A Rising Star	105
Chapter XVIII	The Old Man	114
Chapter XIX	Asmaya	119
Chapter XX	The Unexpected	123
Chapter XXI	The Exodus from Egypt	129

Foreword

It was not in mind, while this book was being written, to recount to my dear reader the story of the prophet Moses (Peace Be Upon Him and upon all God's messengers as well), that most of us, if not all, know his story very well. Though, I consider it, myself, to be the most important event in all mankind history.

Undoubtedly, it is elaborately recounted in many books (the best example is the Holy Qur'an itself) that most of it is, almost, about his story with the Pharaoh and the Children of Israel.

The basic foundation upon which the events of this story take place is that each era has its own great heroes from among the general public, who are not mentioned in history. Although the heroes of this story are created by the author's imagination, they do exist in all eras under different names. As we may know, the people of misfortune are not only the prophets, but also many others that you may see around you. For those are grades of dignity with their Lord, then the company of prophets in Paradise.

Thus, the story here highlights the general public, during the times of prophet Moses, whose lives go in parallel with the big event that has already happened.

Without further prolongation, it is better for my dear reader himself to read, fly with his own imagination, travel a few thousand years back in time, and live with the events of the story.

CHAPTER I

An Evening on the River Nile

As though they had just landed from the high heavens, the wafting breezes glided, flowed lightly, caressed the valley trees, and awakened dewdrops that had fallen into deep sleep since the last night on those trees' leaves. Those dewdrops woke up lazily, fell sluggishly from the top; and picked up by the compassionate River Nile, they embraced it and went with it willingly.

That was a quite minute dot on a very small spot within a *live painting* made by the hand of the Creator Lord.

Somewhere away from this same location—thousands of years ago, where the colour of the sky was different, the smell of the air was different, the taste of things was different—nothing was heard but the hymns of nature and the echo of the nightingale's prayers. In brief, it was the Commission of God on earth.

A small house stood on the outskirts of a village, located on a high hill, a little away from the River Nile, but its windows saw the river very clearly. If you saw that house, you would not overlook the unique taste of its builder. It was not only built from brick, like the other houses in the village, but also from stone. Its walls were covered, both outside and inside, with pieces of stone which varied in their colour and size. It seemed that they were collected from the remains of the building materials of a luxurious palace and were used this way to make a wonderful work of art.

The owner of that wonderful house was a poor young Egyptian man named Hori. He was in his mid-twenties, and lived with his beloved Egyptian wife, the comfort of his eyes: Samatya.

She was nearly twenty. No one who saw her could say anything but that her beauty surpassed even beauty itself. The young men in her village wondered at her beauty, and competed with each other to win her heart. Some confessed their love for her, but she turned all of them down. And some others, who were shy, loved her in silence. They didn't show their feelings for her, so she didn't know anything about their love. She only chose Hori; he was the one she loved.

In fact, that wonderful house they lived in was not their own. They were only allowed by the landowner to build and live in it for a monthly rent of a hundred shaty. The shaty was a unit of currency with an estimated value that evened things out in the familiar barter movement among people at that time, without prejudice to either party. On the other hand, the landowner paid them both three and a half shaty a day for their work on his land. This amount, at that time, was enough to buy a linen robe.

Hori and Samatya worked together in farming during the flood and agriculture seasons, while in the other seasons, Hori worked alone in the field of palace construction. He was much more fond of construction than farming, but the master of that issue was the employer himself, who determined the required number of workers as well as when and where they were needed.

Both of them had to work hard together to provide basic

living expenses, in addition to the necessity of saving to provide the house rent. The landowner was taking almost all their income together for the rent, and leaving them the crumb remnants. They had to manage—and he did not care—otherwise they would be expelled from the house, and deprived of the honour of hard labour in his land, as he was one of the state senior dignitaries at that time.

Anyway, it was what was portioned out for them both by the Lord, the real owner of the whole earth. Also, it was what portioned out for the landowner himself. Truly, it was neither an honour for this landowner, nor a humiliation for those who worked for him, but a trial and test for them all.

Whatever the hardship of life, and whatever the harshness of test and trial was, the same fate with which our misfortune is preordained may bestow upon us, above others, a special gift that outweighs all other things, even if they were the treasures of the whole world.

That special gift can be peace of mind, health of the body, the company of a loving heart, or carefree and calm sleep, even if it was accompanied by the lowest kind of food.

A quiet evening, after a day full of work, brought Hori and Samatya together after they had taken a break for a nap. Sometimes, they would remain awake after their siesta until worktime the next morning, which would usually begin in the latter part of the night, just before the dawn.

These few hours that they spent together were the best time ever in their lives, especially on a calm night like that, and in a place where loving partners would meet alone in private. But the moon was there all night long, and threw its light on Samatya's face so that it became a moon itself. And its light embroidered the River Nile, that it ran like pearl threads amongst the trees, while the breeze sang lullabies by rustling the leaves.

There, in front of their house, they prepared a place for themselves, furnished with a coloured mat made from sugarcane bagasse. They were ensconced together on pillows stuffed with birds' feathers that Samatya had made and embroidered herself in an artistic way. In front of them there were a few pottery dishes of cheese, honey, some fresh vegetables and loaves of the sun bread that had been put in a basket made of palm fronds. There were also two glasses of beer, and close to them was a pottery urn of water as well.

After they finished eating their dinner, they continued their talk that hadn't stopped since their siesta. Their conversations never stopped as long as they were together, as if they were trying to compensate for all that time, as they might think, in which working hours kept them away from each other. Even during the preparation of their dinner they were together hand in hand, and never stopped talking, especially as they were newly married.

In fact, most of the time Samatya was the one who was talking, while Hori kept listening with a smile on his face. It seemed that he did not focus on the details of what she said, but he was busy with her beauty that made him deeply in love with her.

Samatya was talking enthusiastically, in a quick accent about her friend Malissa, whom she met with on her way back home after work. Malissa lived a little further away from their house. She did not work in farming like them, but as a cook in one of the Pharaoh's palaces.

Samatya continued talking to her husband about Malissa, and how she got much more for her work in the Pharaoh's palace compared to what they both earned together.

"Can you imagine, Hori, that she gets five shaty a day for her work there?" she said, while the signs of astonishment were quite clear on Hori's face. "But I wonder why I always see sadness and dissatisfaction in her eyes, despite her luxurious clothes. And she lives a rich life, as she told me herself, compared to ours. I will not hide that I have asked her not to forget me if they were in need of another cook in the palace—because I am a very skilled cook," she added. Then, she concluded proudly with a boasting smile and said, "Of course, you know that, darling, don't you?"

Hori answered with a teasing frown on his face, and said, "Yes … yes, sweetie." Then he added in a lower voice, but he was quite sure that Samatya heard him very well, "I can never say anything else while I'm here on my own with you!" Then they burst out laughing together, as she knew well he always liked to tease her.

The tone of their voices eased, and they got closer to each other. "I'm impatiently waiting for this boy to come," Hori said while putting his hand on her stomach, as she was in her early months of pregnancy.

"And what if she was a girl?" Samatya said.

"A girl or a boy, of course, would be the same for me, sweetie," Hori said, "but truly, I prefer it to be a boy so that he can be a companion of mine, as I've wished since my childhood to have a brother. Also, when he grows up, I wish him to be one of those who are brought near to the god Pharaoh as a priest."

Samatya frowned and moved a little away from him. "What's wrong, Samatya?" Hori said. "Well then, let it be a girl, but do not be angry, sweetie."

"It did not make me angry, but what angered me was that you want to make our son a slave by serving that man," Samatya replied.

He interrupted her immediately.

"Samatya, how does your tongue dare to say that the Pharaoh, the great god, is a man? Sweetie, I'm afraid you'll anger the gods by talking wrongly about a son of theirs."

She said in an angry tone, "Hori, you know very well my opinion about this matter. We have already talked and argued a lot because of it. I'm still not convinced that the Pharaoh is a god, whatever you say and however you justify it to me, and whatever the people say, and chant those priests' nonsense."

"My sweetie and the comfort of my eyes, I'll ask the gods to forgive you," he said in a quiet tone. "It won't make me happy seeing you tormented in the life hereafter because you disbelieve in the great god Pharaoh."

Samatya got angry and continued arguing with him in a voice choked with tears. She said, "You know very well that I am not a disbeliever. I do believe in one god only, who created me, created you, and created your pharaoh. My god is the sun only. And if the god wanted to beget, as those priests claim, he would beget another sun or a star, not a human being like you and me!!"

Hori kept silent, looking sadly towards the river, and did not answer her back. He and Samatya, both kept looking in different directions, in silence, for a long time. Then she got closer to him in an attempt to erase his anger. She calmly smiled and put her hands on his shoulders and said, "I have a wonderful neutral idea!"

He looked at her, silently, in a way as if he was asking her about that idea.

"Darling, you pray to your god for me, and I pray to my god for you too, asking for guidance. The true and stronger god will end our dispute in the matter. What do you think, Hori?" she added.

Hori's face was wreathed with a cheerful smile that wiped out all his grief. He cupped Samatya's cheeks with both hands while his eyes wandered over her face, and said, "It seems that my love and passion for you are not only for your beauty, Samatya, but also for your wisdom."

CHAPTER II

Inside the Pharaoh's Palace

The river continued its journey without stopping or resting, wandering through the good land, quenching its thirst, and telling its stories. Each spot passed by was more beautiful than the previous one. What about the one that was said to be the most wonderful spot ever?

There was the most beautiful place ever, that all other places envied for its unique charm, and how lucky it was. But, at that time, it became the most miserable one of them all—just like a bride who had married someone who was not worthy of her—as it was selected from among all the spots for establishing a palace. The builders excelled in design and construction, with all their knowledge, to make something which befitted a god. (As they also excelled in believing in him, and stooped to him willingly and *un*willingly.) There was the Pharaoh's palace.

It was midday. Far away, within sight of, but outside the palace, a stylish luxurious waggon, pulled by an army of horses, was heading forward as part of a majestic procession. It was surrounded by many other waggons, that were less distinctive and smaller, that were carrying soldiers who whipped anyone who hindered that procession, human being or animal, as in such a situation, both were alike. Also, anyone who ever thought to stop the procession might be killed at once.

As soon as the procession approached the palace gate, it was opened wide immediately by guards who lined up on both sides with their faces almost touching the ground in humble and meek submission, while the sound of the trumpet announced to those inside the palace the arrival of the procession, and to be prepared in turn.

The luxurious waggon passed through the gate, which closed immediately after it had entered. The other accompanying waggons stayed outside the palace.

The waggon headed towards the inner door of the palace, a distance which took quite some time, amid the dense shadows of trees, most of those trees were brought from the land of Punt.

Finally, the waggon arrived and stopped adjacent to the first steps to the entrance door. All those ceremonies were not for the Pharaoh himself, but for one of his daughters, who wanted to stroll outside the palace.

The Pharaoh's daughter got off the waggon. She was just ten years old, and surrounded by a group of chaperones, headed by their chief, who were waiting for the young princess.

On her way to the inner stairs, she complained of the exhausting stroll, as if she had wandered the globe on her feet. Also, she gave instructions to the chief chaperone for her lunch.

The floors and walls of the palace, which were covered with the finest marble and granite, reflected the echo of her voice, until it faded out as she was still giving another instruction; this time, to provide her with a sedan chair to carry her to her room because of the distance. Finally, she reached her room, and at the same time everyone everywhere she passed by heaved a sigh of relief.

After quite some time, the young princess went out of the bathroom, surrounded by her chaperones—with their smiley mummified faces as if they had been frozen in time—when the little princess called to them to not frown in front of her.

Suddenly, she cried out, calling the chief chaperone who came in a hurry. "How many times have I told you before not to bring the food while I'm here? How many times have I told you that I want to find it ready in front of me when I come out of the bathroom?" she said angrily in a loud, echoing voice.

The chief chaperone got very confused while she was focusing her eyes on the food, then she said in a whisper that could hardly be heard, "Your Highness, here is the food waiting for you to have the honour of being tasted and liked by your Highness."

The Pharaoh's daughter got angry and said, "Are you stupid? Don't you understand what I said? They have just brought it now when I came out of the bathroom, but I want it to be ready in front of me: not brought in while I'm coming out of the bathroom. Did you get what I mean? Or have you become an old and senile woman?"

Eventually, it seemed that the chief chaperone got what the Pharaoh's daughter meant. Then she asked permission to leave the room, bowed to her, and kept moving backward until she reached the door; then she disappeared. As soon as she went out of the room, she hurried towards the kitchen like a storm, sweeping aside all workers there, yelling and rebuking them for what had happened, while they were all silent, and looking at each other in fear.

Malissa cut through their silence to try to defend her colleagues who had made the so-called mistake and said,

"Madam, I'm working here as a cook. I know that I have nothing to do with what has happened. But the supervisor of the delivery of food to the rooms complies with your instructions. None of us dares to violate your instructions, madam. Also, I remember well that her Highness complained before that the food was cold, and she ordered it not to be delivered to her room, but when she comes out of the bathroom. Madam, which is which, please?"

Malissa's words left the chief chaperone unable to answer her; she kept silent, then said quietly but decisively, "Each one of you, resume your work. I'll manage it myself."

CHAPTER III

Hori's Dreams

One day, when days seemed to be all the same, Samatya returned home from her work, exhausted. It seemed that Hori had arrived home before her. This was not a problem, but he looked cheerful with no sign of the fatigue that she used to see upon his face by the end of each day.

"How long have you been here?" she asked him.

It seemed that he was eagerly expecting her arrival. He said in a joyful voice, "Samatya, my lovely wife, our life will change forever. I won't let you go to work any more. We'll own a more beautiful house than this. It will be ours, Samatya. And I will …"

Samatya interrupted him. She looked unhappy at what she'd heard.

"What did you say?" she asked. "Tell me, first, how long have you been here? Did you leave your work?"

Hori answered her, but his cheerfulness faded a little as she did not share it with him, and he said, "Yes, I left my work, because what I heard today made me decide not to go to *that* work again."

She looked very tired, especially as she had not taken any rest since early morning, and said, "Tell me quickly, please. I cannot stand any more."

He pulled her closer to him and said, "Well, be seated,

darling. I'll tell you the details of everything. In brief, I will travel to the south with those who were selected to build a new temple there for the great Pharaoh." Then he continued, and said, "I'll prepare lunch myself, sweetie. You just sit, relax, and watch me. Today you'll eat what I cooked myself. I came back home early and made you a kidney beans dish. You have never eaten anything like it before."

Samatya smiled, and calmed down a little. Why not? She'd got rid of that burden of preparing lunch as she was quite tired.

Hori prepared a place for their lunch, then poured the kidney beans from the cooking pot into the dishes, and brought bread as well as fresh lettuce, watercress and radish. In the meantime, he was telling Samatya the details of his intended trip to the south, and said, "I have been preparing for this trip for a long time. I didn't want to inform you about it until after I'd made sure that I was selected. As you know, sweetie, here we work hard the whole month, uselessly, but working there in building that temple, I will get seven shaty a day. In addition, they provide food and residence for all the workers."

He continued talking; hardly eating, himself, but Samatya seemed to be very hungry. She ate quickly till she finished up her food, had some water, and then she attended to him. "Carry on," she said.

"Did you like the kidney beans?" Hori asked.

She looked as if she had forgotten that she had just eaten kidney beans. "Yes, yes, they were delicious. Carry on. I'm listening," she replied.

Hori realised from her facial expression what was in her mind.

"Of course, sweetie, I will miss you a lot," he said. "I would never think of moving away from you but for our difficult circumstances. I wish I could take you with me. Anyway, as soon as I get there, I will do my best to be back together with you as quickly as possible."

It seemed that what Hori said encouraged Samatya to accept his idea even if she did not like it at the beginning. She said, "I don't want to put out the candle of your cheerfulness. I know very well your eagerness to work in the construction field, as well as your hatred of farm work. I would be very happy to be together anywhere, even in the hot weather of the south, but not to be away from each other. I'll pray to god for you to succeed in what you seek for, to come back to me safe and sound, and never be away from each other again."

The joy returned to his voice, and he said, "Rest assured, sweetie, that I'll go out and come back with the blessings of the great Pharaoh, and all our wishes will come true."

Samatya got a little bit angry when she heard what Hori said, but it was not the time to argue about the deity of the Pharaoh. Then they prepared themselves for their siesta.

Samatya fell asleep quickly, while Hori stayed beside her, awake, drawing his daydreams for the near future, and a smile of hope was upon his face.

CHAPTER IV

A Hard Night

The days passed quickly, and Hori has already travelled to the south, while Samatya, alone, tried to recover from the wound of the day of farewell. She moved on, and resumed her life as usual. She went to her work and returned home, but with much more pain and difficulty as she was missing Hori by her side.

One day, after over two months had elapsed, she was surprised by a knocking on her door. She rose up with joy; it ought to be Hori, come home for his vacation. He hadn't told her about the time of his vacation, as he himself didn't know at that time.

But it wasn't Hori. It was a man, accompanied by a woman, whom Samatya later learned was his wife. He worked with Hori in the south; he had come for his vacation, and would be back again. Hori had sent a verbal message with him to reassure Samatya that he was alright, and asking her to leave her work. Also, he sent her three hundred shaty in order to pay the house rent and to spend from the remaining amount. And if he could not come home soon for his vacation, he would send her a message as well as to when he *would* be able to.

The two guests left Samatya overwhelmed by her conflicting feelings and thoughts, as if all the colours of sadness and happiness were mingled together upon her face like a sad painting, of which the master colour was tears.

Then, the days passed much too sluggishly; and although she was able to leave behind the misery of work in farming, the misery of loneliness and bewilderment became her new companion.

One day, as usual, the representative of the landowner passed by to collect the house rent. He knocked on her door, and Samatya opened it to pay him. He asked her about Hori and, of course, did not forget to ask her about herself too, meanwhile blaming her husband, and asking how could he leave her alone like that, especially since she was a pretty woman.

"It is none of your business. You got your rent. Now go away from here," she said angrily and slammed the door in his face.

He left, hiding something for her deep inside himself.

The same evening, after all other eyes were asleep in the quiet of the night, Samatya's eyes were still awake, overwhelmed by the misery of her loneliness. She opened her door and went out of the house, looking towards the sky as if she was looking for her sun, in whom she used to confide; but she did not find it. When she saw the moonlight, her eyes flooded with tears and started to complain to the moon.

Then she sat on the ground, drew her knees close to her chest, and leaned her cheek on her crossed arms, while fear and sadness fought together in her eyes. Then tears proclaimed sadness was the winner.

Samatya heard a sneaking sound coming from amongst the trees. Then she saw a shadow move stealthily in the dark, and start to run quickly towards her. She rose up at once, frightened, and rushed towards the house. No sooner had she entered the house than he pushed her inside and shut the door upon them both.

Her screams and shouts echoed all over the place, helplessly seeking out an ear to hear, but there was nothing at all; then they rose up to the sky, while he sought to seduce her. Then she twisted herself free from his grip, and he ran after her. Eventually she eluded him, picked up a knife, and all at once she turned back to him and pointed the knife towards his face.

He froze in his place, then he slowly moved backward.

"If you dare to move just one step forward I will stab you in the heart," Samatya said in a threatening, angry tone, with eyes wide open.

He remained in his place for a while. (He was the representative of the landowner who had passed by earlier that day.) He tried to convince himself that she wouldn't dare to carry out her threat; she wouldn't gamble with her reputation, and she would finally give in to him. And if she complained to the landowner, he wouldn't believe her either.

Suddenly, he attacked her once again. But she overtook him with her stabs, with all the strength she had, driven by her anger, a feeling of oppression, injustice, and the pain of the years of her life all together. She fulfilled her threat that he thought she would never dare to. He fell down on the ground, fighting death, then stretched out on his back unmoving, and finally he died.

Although Samatya realised the horrible fact that she had become a murderer, she did not feel guilty. If he returned to life again a thousand times she would kill him each and every time, again and again, the same way without any regret. But it was frightening to her, the idea of how she would be doomed.

Surely she might be killed when people found out that she had murdered the representative of the landowner. The first accusation that might come to their minds was that she killed him to steal the money that was in his possession. Masters were always right, and their justifications were acceptable, even if they were wrong; while poor people were always guilty, none of their justifications were acceptable, and might be used against them too, even if they were the victims.

Despite the crime being horrible, it put out the fire of her anger. She felt the victory of good over evil. Not only did Samatya see that good prevails, she also did it with her own hands. But, what would be the price?

At first, Samatya seemed to be acting as if nothing happened. She changed her clothes that were stained with his dirty blood, and washed her hands. When she saw his body stretched on the ground, on her way out, she felt sick and spat on him. Then, she went out of the house calmly, and shut the door upon him.

No sooner had she seen the moon up in the sky staring at her with a wide-open eye—as if it was watching her and had come tonight for her only—than she burst out crying.

There was the truth that shocked her, that she had never thought about before so seriously as she did at that time. Where was the sun, her god? Did it know what had happened to her? Did it know that she was innocent? But how, while it was absent? Would the moon inform it? But when, and how?

Samatya's fear of people increased greatly after this horrible conclusion. She had a strong and urgent need for a god to protect her from it; a god who knew the truth of what had happened—that she was defending herself. Then, surely, he would protect her and she would never be scared of people any more, even if they were unjust to her. It would be quite enough for her to feel that god was well pleased with her, even if *they* considered her a murderer.

But, where was that god? The sun that she had been worshipping for a long time was absent, and wouldn't believe her the next day—that she was innocent, whatever she would swear.

Samatya started sobbing her heart out and screaming; an echoing sound that climbed up to the sky, while the rest of the place was dead silent. Anyone who might have seen her like that at that moment, and know what she had done, might think that she had lost her mind. It did not matter whether she was wrong or right. The point was that the bloodshed itself was quite enough to make anyone lose their mind, especially a sensitive woman like her. But the truth was that she had never been in full command of her reason other than at that time.

She asked herself, "Did that happen to me because I disbelieved in the Pharaoh, and did not glorify him like Hori does?" Then she started crying again when she remembered Hori. She wished he was there by her side at that moment. Then she asked herself again, "But where is Hori now, and where is the Pharaoh himself?"

Eventually she realised that she was quite alone there, and nobody knew about her catastrophe. She raised her eyes towards the sky and prayed in a voice choked with tears that could be hardly understood.

"O my Lord, my God, O You who created me, O You who created everything. Where are You? Who are You? Guide me to You. Protect me. Show me what to do. Nobody knows but You, nobody saw me but You, nobody knows my reasons but

You. O Lord, guide me to You, give me a sign to assure me who You are. Are you the sun? Are you the moon? Are you the stars? Or who are you then? O Lord, O Lord, O Lord."

After some time she was about to fall asleep; but she had slept already for a while, and then quickly woke up as if having slept for a very long time. It was still night. She raised her eyes again towards the sky as if she was looking for the answer. She neither saw the moon nor the stars, as though all the sky was covered with dark clouds. There was nothing at all to see.

Suddenly, Samatya came to her senses, and checked on the dead body still stretched out inside the house. Fear crept back into her soul; she got up, frightened, and rushed towards her friend Malissa's house, which was some way off. She ran across the dark fields, looked behind her every now and then in horror; then tumbled down, got up again, and resumed her way without stopping for a rest.

The dogs' barking was getting closer to her. She increased her speed more and more. Then her feet slipped, and she rolled down a small hill. She got up again quickly and ran faster.

Finally, Malissa's house came into view. She started crying again until she arrived, and kept knocking on the door with both hands repeatedly while she looked behind her in fear. Then Samhari, Malissa's husband, opened up, with a look of shock on his face when he saw her like that, and Malissa behind him, both having woken up in panic. Samatya was completely drained of energy and she fell down, unconscious.

Malissa and her husband carried Samatya to a room inside their house. Samhari grasped Malissa's arm, pulled her out of the room, and whispered to her, "She must leave immediately after she wakes up. We don't know what she has done, and we don't need any trouble."

Malissa said angrily, "Didn't you see her? Does she look as if she has done something, or that something might have happened to her?"

"Didn't you spot the blood on her clothes? She might have killed someone," Samhari answered.

Malissa became very worried and hurried to check Samatya, as she hadn't really noticed any blood on her clothes—only mud—and tried to wake her up. She left the room, went and got something, and ran back again inside in a hurry. After some time, she came out crying and carrying a small roll of cloth.

"This is what she has killed, as you claimed. Will you bury it, or shall I go myself?" Malissa said.

Samhari looked down sadly, and slowly took the roll from her in order to bury it.

The sun rose and dispelled the darkness from the whole village so that all its features became clear. By that time, Samatya had already told Malissa all about what happened to her the previous night.

In the meantime, life returned to the whole village, while Samhari was digging a grave for the foetus. Whoever passed by, if they asked him about what he was doing, he told them what had happened to Samatya, his wife's friend; and then the news began to spread all over the village.

"What you have just told me now, nobody must know about whatsoever, apart from you and me," Malissa whispered to Samatya.

"I'm so scared, Malissa. I don't know what to do," Samatya said while still crying.

"Leave it up to me, Samatya," Malissa whispered to her confidently. "Just remember what I have said to you, and no one will know what has happened except you and me. All they should know is that you felt severe pain last night and came here for help, and the rest as you know."

CHAPTER V

Malissa and Samatya

Samhari came back after he had buried the foetus. At the same time, Malissa came out of the room where she left Samatya tired. Malissa was silent, a severe sadness on her face.

Samhari got close to her and apologised in a low, quiet voice for what he had said last night.

"Don't say you are sorry," Malissa whispered to him. "Forget it. All that I need from you is just to bring us a waggon, for me and her, to take us to her house whenever she wakes up. I will stay there with her for a couple of days to be reassured that she is recovered. Also, I don't want to disturb you here. You just take care of our children till I come back."

After a short silence, he said, "What about your work?"

She replied angrily, in a sharp whispering voice. "She has nobody to take care of her but me, and I need to have some rest from that work even for just two days, as it suffocates me. Anyway, if you are worried about those two days, I will pay them back from my savings."

Samhari quickly told her not to worry, and reassured her that he would do whatever she wanted. On the same day, before sunset, he rented a waggon to take Malissa and Samatya to Samatya's house.

Upon their arrival, they both paused, as if frozen, for a while in front of the house before going inside. "We have to finish up quickly, then wait till nightfall to do what I told you about," Malissa said. Samatya agreed with all Malissa said, and complied with her completely.

Samatya opened the door, then they entered together cautiously, holding onto each other, walking on tiptoe as if they were afraid to wake him up from a nap. They had brought a big sack and a long length of rope.

"Before we close the sack, we need some heavy stones to put inside with the body," Malissa said.

They went out of the house and brought some back, put the body inside the sack with the stones, and then closed it tightly. They moved it with difficulty to a corner of the house, then painstakingly cleaned the place of any traces which might indicate that a murder had been committed there.

The sun had already set by then. They went out of the house, and sat together silently, holding onto each other, waiting for the right time. After quite a while, they looked around everywhere to make sure that nobody was there. Then they went back inside the house, and together dragged the sack painfully and with great effort out of the house and all the way to the edge of the hill. They pushed it together with their feet down into the river. No sooner had they pushed it than they heard the splash; then it disappeared, causing a whirlpool in the river which mirrored the disruption it had caused in the two friends' lives. "Go to hell!" they said both together angrily, and tired. They hugged each other and cried.

"You have done me a huge favour," Samatya said. "I owe you my life, Malissa."

"Don't say that, Samatya," Malissa said. "I consider you a sister, not just a friend. I will be here with you till you and I are both assured that you are all right."

Malissa knew that she had to help prepare Samatya psychologically to recover quickly from what had happened, as she would have to return home to her children and husband sooner or later. Also, Samatya had to manage till Hori came back, and then have to convince him to move to a new house.

After a brief silence, Malissa said, "Samatya, you have to change your routine temporarily until Hori comes back, like staying awake by night and sleeping by day. Also, you might put a curtain outside the house, to sleep behind and for privacy, instead of sleeping inside the house, as it is difficult for you right now to sleep alone inside."

"I hate this house and the whole place itself. Even the river scares me," Samatya said.

"It's just a matter of time, darling. Tomorrow you won't remember anything about it," Malissa said. Then she tried to change the conversation to take Samatya's mind off that horrible event.

"Let me tell you what happened two days ago in the Pharaoh's palace," Malissa said. Then she told Samatya about the Pharaoh's spoiled daughter, who didn't know what she wanted and caused much trouble for all the people around her. Then Samatya and Malissa tried, with difficulty, to smile. But their smile didn't match the way they were feeling.

As they sat outside together on a mat in front of the house, Samatya leaned back and laid her head on Malissa's lap. Malissa was sitting relaxed, resting her back against the wall.

"Tell me more about your work, Malissa," Samatya said.

"What do you want to know?" Malissa answered.

"About people there, what you like, what you don't like. Truly, I want to know if you are happy in your work or not," Samatya replied.

Malissa kept silent for a while, then she sighed and said, "I can't deny that I get paid quite a bit there, but at the same time there are many workfellows whose faces I hate to look at ... and ..." Suddenly she stopped talking.

"And what?" Samatya asked.

"Injustice and oppression, Samatya," Malissa replied in a voice full of sadness. "I didn't mean myself. I know well how to deal with and get my own rights. But I meant other people, who are humiliated and insulted as if they were not human beings like us."

Samatya raised herself up, got closer, and tucked her hands under Malissa's arm as it was getting colder as the night wore on. "Why don't they defend themselves?" she said.

Malissa smiled and said, "Sometimes you seem so naïve, and don't know anything of life, but because I know you very well and how you think, it seems to me by this so-called naïvety that you're gradually trying to lead me into something I don't understand."

Samatya smiled softly, and said, "Then tell me the truth frankly and I promise to stop my so-called naïvety."

Malissa laughed, briefly went quiet, then began talking in a wondering sad tone, as if she was asking Samatya for an answer.

"There is a woman who works in the kitchen as a cleaner. She cleans the floors, throws the garbage out of the palace, and work like that."

Samatya was listening with interest, and asked Malissa to carry on.

Malissa resumed. "That woman is quiet and friendly She always tries to reach out to everyone there. But most of them treat her harshly. For me, I don't like their attitude, though

I myself, at the beginning, felt like there was a barrier between me and her, but I have never treated her like them whatsoever.

Samatya asked with sympathy, "Why do they treat her like that?"

"Just because she is one of the Children of Israel," Malissa answered.

"Yes, I heard about them, but I don't know much," Samatya said.

"Those who are the followers of Joseph, who lived here in Egypt a long time ago, and they believe that he was a prophet. Also they deny that the Pharaoh is a god, but they don't say it publicly. And they say that there is only one God who selects his Messengers from among human beings to convey His message to all other people. And ..." Malissa said, and suddenly stopped.

"Carry on, Malissa," Samatya said with interest.

"I don't know much more," Malissa said. "But it bewilders me that, although she is treated in a bad way, she never thinks to change her attitude towards those who hurt her, even after all she had been through before."

"It is getting more complicated for me. I really don't understand. What is behind your interest in that woman, Malissa?" Samatya asked.

Malissa seemed to be awkward, and said, "Nothing at all. It just hurts me that they treat her like that."

"What is her name?" Samatya asked.

"Rachel," Malissa answered, and suddenly fell silent for quite some time.

"What is wrong, Malissa?" Samatya asked.

Malissa turned her face and looked in the other direction. With her hand, Samatya turned Malissa's face towards her again, while Malissa was trying to hide her tears from Samatya.

Samatya hugged her and said, "Malissa, tell me what's wrong. There is something you are hiding from me. Why don't you tell me the truth? After all you have done for me, don't you want me even to share your grief, at least?"

Many more tears were Malissa's answer.

Then they stayed the whole night till the first hours of the next morning talking about Rachel, as Samatya asked Malissa to tell her the whole story. It seemed that Samatya's curiosity about Rachel made her forget, temporarily, the previous hard night.

"Rachel is over sixty, a very poor woman; more than you can imagine, Samatya," Malissa said. "You would consider us very rich compared to her. She lost her newly born twins—they were all she had—and lost her husband as well."

"How did that happen?" Samatya asked.

"They were all killed by the Pharaoh's soldiers," Malissa replied.

"But why?" Samatya asked.

"First, her twins were killed that year in which all newly born males had to be killed, and …" said Malissa.

Samatya interrupted her and said, "Malissa, do you believe in all that people say? It is not logical that the Pharaoh would order to kill young babies, and for what? People always like to start rumours for no reason at all."

Malissa replied angrily, "I have been working in the Pharaoh's palace for quite a period of time. I know what you don't know, Samatya. Those people who suffered from such oppression and humiliation were weak, and no one helped them. The other people not only didn't care about them, but also claimed that they deserved what they had been through."

At that moment, Samatya sensed the truth of what Malissa said. Then, thirsty to know the whole truth, she said, "Tell me everything you know, Malissa."

Malissa recounted to Samatya the story of the Pharaoh and the prophecy of an approaching birth of one who would threaten his throne; also, that his kingdom would be vanquished because of this child from the Children of Israel. The Pharaoh was terrified, and ordered that all the newly born males of the Children of Israel be killed immediately.

At that time, Rachel gave birth to twins, and when the Pharaoh's soldiers came and invaded their houses as usual, her husband intercepted them, trying to dissuade them from doing what they were sent to do, begged them to leave his twins, and to kill him instead. They threw him to the ground while he kept begging the soldiers to let him at least keep just one of the twins.

There was no answer given by the soldiers except that they slaughtered both of the twins before him. Then they turned and killed him as well even as he cried out, expressing his anger at such injustice. All the while, Rachel watched helplessly.

Malissa ended the story and burst into tears, while Samatya sobbed and remembered all her grief.

She deeply thought and compared herself to Rachel. She had lost her foetus, while Rachel witnessed the slaughter of her twins. Hori travelled away from her, while Rachel's husband was slaughtered before her eyes as well.

Then, she remembered what was behind all this. She remembered that she disbelieved in the Pharaoh as a god. And after she heard that horrible story from Malissa, her hatred for the Pharaoh greatly increased. As well as that, she remembered what happened to her on that hard night. She rose up on her knees and yelled angrily in an echoing voice, "Woe to you, Pharaoh."

Malissa stopped her by blocking her mouth with her hand, and looked around for fear that somebody would hear her, especially now that it was sunrise, and whispered sharply, "Samatya, are you crazy?"

Samatya moved Malissa's hand roughly away from her mouth, and continued by crying out, "The craziness is to believe such a Pharaoh to be a god."

Malissa, helpless, could no longer control her.

"O, Pharaoh," Samatya yelled in the same echoing voice, "if you are truly a god, then hear me now. Come and kill me because I disbelieve in you. Do you hear me? I disbelieve in you!" Then she fell down exhausted, panting, and Malissa was hugging and comforting her.

After a while, some soldiers on a waggon approached. Samatya looked at Malissa in panic, with eyes wide open, as if she was asking her, *Did the Pharaoh hear me?*

The waggon got closer, then one of the soldiers got off, greeted them, and asked, "Did anyone of you see the representative of the landowner?"

"Yes, I saw him yesterday the first, in the morning. He came to collect the house rent as usual," Samatya replied firmly and confidently.

Malissa looked at Samatya in admiration of her confidence and what she said.

As he was about to leave, the soldier said, "Well, I hope you will let us know immediately if you get any news," and left.

The waggon stopped again not far away from them. It seemed that the same soldier was asking someone who was passing by. After that, the waggon continued on its way.

Samatya and Malissa watched them silently till they had disappeared. Then, they both burst out laughing, hugging each other as they had succeeded, and their fear had finally left them.

Their happiness vanished quickly and was replaced by sadness again. It seemed that Rachel's shadow still hovered over everything, and might stay for a long time. No one could say.

CHAPTER VI

In the South

The North and the South, if we had to compare them, would be like two beautiful girls that could catch any eye: the first of them with a quiet soft beauty, and the other one's beauty different, perhaps because of having thicker eyebrows or a taller body.

Here, in the South and far away from the North, where the river was still beginning its journey, it was more spacious and more generous than in the North, so that it bestowed more fertility and more strength on the lands around it. Even the sun itself seemed to be bigger here, as if it might also have fallen in love with the South, which brought it nearer to it so that the South got much hotter weather: the price of that nearness.

On the west bank of the river there was a huge mountain that had been selected to establish the temple; more precisely, out of which the temple would be carved. Thousands of workers and technicians were deployed all over the worksite, each knowing his role. Each group of them had a supervisor, and the supervisors had a chief supervisor. All of them worked under the supervision of a group of architects. This hierarchy carried out the instructions of the chief architect, who set the location and designed the temple himself.

Every now and then, he had to come to the worksite to

follow up the implementation of his instructions to the letter. He did not accept any mistake; he was very strict and precise. When he was attending the worksite, nothing was heard but whispers. Why not? He was a relative of the Pharaoh himself and was assigned by him to establish that temple.

The worksite was still in the process of preparation; workers were removing large outcrops of the mountain which were impeding the implementation of the design.

Hori was just one among thousands of workers. He was enjoying his work since he had arrived a few months ago. The pressure of his work made him to forget that days were passing, but never made him forget Samatya. He was always thinking about her; she was motivating him as if he was building that temple for her. Many times, during his work, a clear smile appeared on his face when he remembered their talks together.

His smile became bigger when he remembered what they once said to each other.

"Samatya, sweetie and the comfort of my eyes, I wish I could carve a lofty palace for you, darling, out of the highest mountain in the world, that would overshadow the Great Pyramid of Cheops," he had said.

"Hori, darling, I don't want you to cut the mountain for me; just cut this water melon; I'm so exhausted," Samatya had said, and they burst out laughing together.

One day, the chief architect came to the site to inspect the initial progress of the work. Everyone was busy, each in his role. He was dictating his instructions standing on the same level of the mountain that Hori was standing on.

Hori was busy in his work, but at the same time he was listening with interest to the instructions the chief architect gave to the junior architects, as if he wanted to learn with them too.

While he was cracking the rock, a handful of sand fell on him from above. The chief architect was still dictating his instructions to the others on the same level, and all the people around him were deadly silent. Also, the entire site was in dead silence but for the sound of tools and cracking.

Hori looked up to determine where the sand which had fallen on him came from. He saw a huge rock on the verge of falling. He cried out to alert everyone there. The chief architect heard the panic in Hori's cry, but he froze in his place, not understanding what was going on.

There was no time for Hori to explain. He rushed towards the chief architect, hugged him and pushed him out of the way of the rock, which had by now fallen and crushed the temple's first victims. He and the chief architect rolled and fell together down the mountain, while he protected the chief architect by taking the roughest blows from the rocks on *his* body.

The chief architect stood up, stunned by what had happened. He only had minor scratches, and he felt very grateful to this brave and faithful worker who had saved him from certain death, but the crowd around him did not give him a chance even to thank Hori. They rushed towards him to be reassured, and to congratulate him on having been saved.

While Hori was one of those who were stretched on the ground, unmoving and covered in blood, that nobody paid attention to.

CHAPTER VII

Among the Children of Israel

Samatya and Malissa fell deep asleep after the soldiers had left. Although the sun was high in the sky, they had no desire to wake up. But the sun had a different desire. Thus, it sent its rays on a mission to awaken them. They both resisted to start with, and tried to remain sleepy, but it was not to be: they were forced to wake up sluggishly—and realised that it was midday.

Both of them were preoccupied by one question, yet they didn't disclose it to each other. But, both of them knew it at the same time when they both looked towards the river with interest. Then they smiled at each other that they had done the same thing at the same time, spontaneously. The most important thing was that they both received the answer from the river, that it was still flowing and keeping their secret from the previous night; and if one day its waters felt straitened by their secret, its crocodiles would be more than able to keep it forever.

Sometimes days seemed to be similar, as if they were all born from the same womb, but that day was quite different from the previous one in that the two friends were obviously active, they shared each other in making their food, and didn't stop talking about anything and everything.

Samatya didn't stop thinking about Rachel and what she

had been through. At the same time she was thinking about herself too. She didn't forget that Malissa would return to her own house, and leave her in this horrible place which once was a heaven. She seemed to be strong and to not care, but the idea that she would be alone frightened her too much. She tried to wipe out the thought, but it seemed to keep reminding her.

Malissa didn't overlook this, but she couldn't find any solution, as she was also thinking about the same thing that Samatya was preoccupied with. It seemed that the two friends were reading each other's minds.

Samatya got an idea that was born out of two other ideas: the first, her sympathy for Rachel; and the second one being that she was frightened to be alone, especially not knowing when Hori would return from the south. Thus, her idea was to bring Rachel to live with her.

Immediately, Samatya disclosed her idea to Malissa, and asked her if Rachel would accept coming to live with her. Malissa liked the idea very much, and reassured Samatya that Rachel would of course agree to come, as she was a lonely woman, needed good company, and would never find a better place anywhere else but with her.

Samatya was much pleased and said, "I will also get her to leave her work. She will then be here only; with me."

Malissa hugged her for that idea too, and she heaved a sigh of relief as Samatya comforted her. She had been very worried thinking about how Samatya would be after she had returned home.

"Why should we wait? Why don't we go today and bring her?" Samatya said.

"Then let's go right now, so that we can get back before

sunset. Her house is not nearby," Malissa replied.

They got up together, intending to go to Rachel's house, which was in a nearby village in the Children of Israel's neighbourhood. The two friends walked together, and tried to stop a waggon to take them to where they were heading, but most waggoners refused disdainfully, and resumed their way.

Finally, after quite some time, they found a waggoner who agreed but for an increased fare. Samatya immediately rushed to get on the waggon, but Malissa prevented her while still talking to the waggoner.

"Well, all right, but you have to wait for us there for a while in order to bring us back here again," Malissa said.

"The fare will be quite different then. It will be double," the waggoner said.

The two friends looked at each other, and got on. "Hurry up, then. We have to come back before sunset," Malissa said to the waggoner.

The waggon moved off quickly.

After quite some time they reached their destination. Samatya looked around at the houses and people there, and realised that this was the first time she had ever been there.

"Stop here, and wait for us," Malissa said.

The two friends got off the waggon and walked a little towards Rachel's house. It was clear that Malissa knew the place very well, but Samatya's eyes were examining the place with shock and sadness upon her face because everything there reflected severe poverty. There were primitive mud houses, and people with eyes full of oppression and misery. Everyone who passed by the two friends looked at them as if they had both landed on them from the sky.

Finally, they reached Rachel's house. Malissa knocked

on the door, which was half closed. Rachel soon appeared, and warmly welcomed Malissa. No sooner had she spotted Samatya behind Malissa than she smiled at her, and said to Malissa, while still looking at Samatya, "If I knew that you had sisters, I would say that she is your sister, as she looks so much like you, Malissa."

Samatya stepped forward and greeted her as she was looking and smiling at her too.

Samatya seemed to be surprised by Rachel's features; she had rather expected something else. Although Rachel was an old woman, she was still beautiful, and the traces of aging increased her gravitas. She was blonde, had eyes as blue as a clear sky but which were deeply sad as if grief had occupied them for decades. She was slim and tall, wearing a cloak over a garment, and though her dark grey clothes were humble, she looked elegant.

Blushing, she said, "I would like to welcome you, but the place ..."

The two friends interrupted her, apologising that they had come unexpectedly, and not really for an ordinary visit. They explained why they had come.

Some time later, the two friends got back into the waggon, on their way home. Between them sat Rachel with a small bundle of clothes: everything that she possessed.

CHAPTER VIII

Rachel and Samatya

The waggon stopped by Malissa's house on their way back home. She climbed down and saw them both off, and promised to meet them again, if possible. The waggon resumed its way towards Samatya's house until it arrived safely. The sun, meanwhile, gathered up the remains of its day, and brought the promise of a new one.

"I hope you like the place, mother," Samatya said.

"The place is wonderful, dear daughter, just because you are here, but all places are the same for me," Rachel replied.

Samatya smiled, and said, "Your words make me so happy, mother."

Rachel smiled back at her, and patted her hand. Then, she prepared a place for Rachel inside the house and put her bundle there.

"Take some rest, mother, and I'll prepare a place for us outside the house, and make some food to eat together as I'm starving," Samatya said. She smiled again and added, "I promise, I'll make you a very special meal tomorrow, to really let you taste my cooking."

Rachel quietly smiled at her and patted her hand again. Then she sat outside the house waiting for Samatya.

After a while, Samatya came with some food, sat before Rachel, put the food between them both, and said, "Come on, mother; to eat together."

Rachel stretched out her hand and whispered, "In the name of God, the most Gracious, the most Merciful." Samatya listened to what she said. She heard it clearly, and was about to ask her about it, but she did not want to distract her from eating, so she kept it to herself for the time being.

Their supper was quiet and friendly, during which Samatya told her about her life, childhood, husband, her previous work and many other things. Rachel listened to her while she was eating.

"Praise be to God," she said after she had eaten. Then she said, "God bless you, daughter, for this good food."

Then, Samatya couldn't contain her curiosity any more. She smiled at Rachel and asked about what she had said before and after her food.

Rachel quietly and confidently smiled at her and said, "Before starting to eat, I mentioned the name of God over the food for His blessings to be upon it, and after I finished, I thanked God for His grace."

"Who is God, mother?" Samatya asked in a wondering, quiet tone.

Rachel concluded that Samatya had a desire to know the truth, as she knew well that, at that time, the dominant belief was pagan. And if Samatya was convinced and reassured by her pagan belief, she wouldn't ask that question in that way. If her question was just out of curiosity, which of course might happen, she wouldn't ask in such a thirsty tone for the answer.

Rachel smiled tenderly, looked into Samatya's eyes, and said, "God is my Lord, and the Lord of everything, who created me, and created everything."

"Where is He? And *how* is He?" Samatya asked in the

same tone, and with a more thirsting look in her eyes.

"He is everywhere. He is here with us now. He hears and sees us, He is with us wheresoever we may be. We may grasp Him with our hearts, but no vision can grasp Him, while His grasp is over all visions. And there is nothing like unto Him," Rachel replied.

Samatya kept silent for a while and thought about what Rachel had said; and then she asked, "How do hearts grasp Him?"

"I'll give you an example to make it clear for you. If we pray and ask Him for something that nobody knows about except us, and we find what we asked for comes true at that time, our hearts grasp Him in that He exists, hears and sees. Each one of us grasps Him his own way," Rachel replied.

Samatya felt that she needed some time to understand what Rachel had said. She didn't tell her so, but she excused herself to take the empty plates back inside the house, and would come back shortly to resume their talk together.

After some time, Samatya came back and once again warmly welcomed Rachel into her house, and said that she was very pleased with this wonderful evening with her. Then she said, "What you said, mother, makes me want to ask you a lot of questions, but I'm afraid it may be a bother to you. You may need to have some rest."

"The opposite is true, daughter," Rachel said with a warm smile. "I'm pleased with your questions, and it comforts me to answer you."

Rachel's words pleased Samatya, and encouraged her to ask enthusiastically, "Well, I heard about some people who call the others to worship one God who we don't see. Those people call themselves prophets, and that God chose them to convey His message to other people. How can you be sure that they are calling you to the true God?"

"That's right," Rachel said. "The first important step, in order to believe in what those people are calling you to, is to believe in those prophets themselves, and that won't be possible until after you have thought deeply and carefully about what they are calling you to as well."

"More clarification, mother, please," Samatya said.

"Well, if they are inviting you to all that is good, forbidding you from what is evil, and don't ask for a reward for that, then it is logical to believe them," Rachel said.

"If I did as you said; if I called people, invited them to what is good, forbade them from what is evil, and didn't ask for a reward; and I also told them that I was sent to them by a god, but the truth was no god sent me, how would people then know whether I was true or not?" Samatya asked.

"Your question, my daughter, reveals your wisdom and that you are thinking neutrally," Rachel said. "Indeed, the true faith cannot be built but upon a good mind, and what you said is completely right.

"Thus, God supported His prophets with miracles that neither other people nor those who claim to be prophets can come up with. That's why the people of those prophets asked them for a miracle to prove their prophethood and to reassure their hearts.

"Some of those people were sincere in their request and believed when they saw that miracle, while the others remained infidels as they wouldn't believe in miracles whatsoever, and they arrogantly deny what they see and refuse to follow a human being like them. They might wish that the Message had been sent down to *them* instead, or be sent down to a specific one with specific attributes.

"Thus, the truth is that they hate the idea itself; they refuse the authority of Creator God upon them. So they argue and mock, and deep down in their hearts they know well that they won't believe whatever the miracle was.

"Indeed, it is not the prophets themselves that they deny, but the favour of God that they really deny; that they proclaim their disbelief in those prophets while they hide in their hearts their denial of God's favour upon them."

Samatya was listening with great interest, and thinking deeply about what Rachel was saying. Then she asked, "Well, why does not God show Himself to us, like the sun for example, and tell us Himself that He was the one who created us. Then no one can deny or disbelieve."

Rachel smiled and said, "It would be so simple, my dear daughter, if it happened like that. Indeed, all people then would believe exactly the same as you said. But the reason for our existence here on this earth is a test for a certain period of time. The test is the choice to believe or disbelieve willingly, without seeing God. That's why God hid Himself from our sight and became unseen, temporarily. This is the test itself.

"But He didn't hide Himself from our hearts. He let us think, feel and grasp Him with our hearts without seeing Him with our eyes, to reach Him willingly."

Samatya thought about what she had heard from Rachel, remembering and retrieving all her life events, her belief in the sun when it had let her down at a very critical time in her life, and then she was quite sure that it was not worthy to be a god; just as she denied the Pharaoh to be a god, too, as he was just a human being. Also, she thought about her hard night and her prayer, in which she was looking for the real god who created her, who knew all about her, who heard and saw her.

She invoked him to save her from her great distress, then she had been already saved, and her prayer came true.

Also, in the same prayer, she had asked the real god to give her a sign, and to guide her to him. Had that come true too? Was Rachel her guide to him?

Her head became crowded with so many thoughts, she could not decide anything yet. She did not like to rush things as she had before, so as not to be let down again as she had been before by the sun.

Rachel noticed the signs of distraction on Samatya's face, as if she knew what she was thinking of. She interrupted her thoughts and said, "Daughter, fateful things usually are preceded by great bewilderment."

Samatya looked over, and said, "Excuse me, mother, did you say something?"

Rachel repeated what she had said to her.

"Why did you say that?" Samatya said.

"Because I read your face and found many lines full of bewilderment," Rachel replied.

Suddenly, Samatya asked her, "Why is there no prophet amongst us now who comes up with a miracle, mother? I mean, in this time we live in."

"For decades, daughter, people have been saying that his time gets closer, while my life is about to end, and he has never shown himself up to now. Who knows? Anyway, I have never seen, myself, any prophet in my life, but I believed without seeing any one of them."

Samatya prayed and wished her a long life and said, "Really, you've stunned me with all that you've said. Who taught you all that, mother?"

Rachel laughed for the first time and said, "When I was

very young, much younger than you, I was asking my father your same questions, and he answered me like I answered you, so I learned from him."

"And who taught your father?" Samatya asked.

"My grandfather, who, in turn, learned from his father too, till we reach our father Joseph, then Jacob, Isaac, Abraham, and finally the father of all, Adam. All of us belong to him, we are all originally brothers and sisters, but we are different in many things. For example, I'm not as beautiful as you."

Samatya laughed in such a way that all signs of bewilderment on her face were wiped out, and she said, "It's a nice compliment, but where does my beauty compare to yours, mother? I wish I could have eyes like yours."

Rachel laughed and said, "You're really beautiful; you know it very well without anybody telling you so."

Samatya said, "You too, mother. You knew it very well decades before anyone like me told you."

Rachel burst out laughing after she heard Samatya's comment, and said, "I had never laughed like this until after I knew Malissa, then you, daughter."

Samatya said proudly and tenderly, "Malissa told me a lot about you, mother; how great and wonderful you are."

Rachel's smile faded as Samatya's tone of voice reflected the hard trial that Rachel had been through.

Samatya watched what she said, and quickly resumed. "I feel like as if you *are* my mother. I don't feel lonely with you any more, and through your wisdom I will try to get a clear vision."

Rachel hugged her and said, "I'll pray to my Lord for you, daughter, and I do really consider myself your mother. Do you agree?"

Samatya's eyes flooded with tears. It was her answer.

CHAPTER IX

Aborted Dreams

The discussion between Rachel and Samatya started to quieten down gradually, till dead silence left Samatya preoccupied with her thoughts; which Rachel clearly noticed so she had to leave her alone talking to herself. Rachel excused herself, and went to sleep in the place Samatya had prepared for her inside, while Samatya remained outside the house.

Although their conversation had long since ended, it was still echoing noisily in Samatya's head. She felt somewhat scared for a while, sitting in *that* place, but soon she remembered that Rachel was there, so she smiled, felt grateful for her presence, and resumed thinking about all that she had said.

She let her eyes drift towards the horizon, going through its distant page-like layers, as if she was trying to read some lines from the future. She remained thus until she didn't know whether she was asleep or still awake. Then she spotted, far away, a rippling white sail cleaving the darkness of the night, and it was slowly getting closer. It was a large boat, sailing northwards on the river. She could clearly see a crowd of people on that boat—they might be soldiers—while the boat got much closer, and docked nearby.

Samatya's heart almost stopped, watching as one of them gets off the boat and rushes swiftly towards her. In a blink of an eye, she stood up, frightened, ran inside the house, closed the door and stood behind it, holding her breath. She turned, and walked towards Rachel's room to wake her up, but suddenly changed her mind once again, and returned to the door. She tried cautiously to listen to what was happening outside. The footsteps were getting closer and louder, but not louder than Samatya's heartbeats.

Samatya was scared to death when she heard quick knocks on the door, but opened it up without thinking as soon as she heard the password. It was just Hori's voice, calling her by the pet name he used to call her by that nobody else knew but both of them. He told her he'd come back, asked her to open up the door, and not to be scared.

She yelled his name cheerfully and rushed to meet him, so strongly that she almost fell out of the house, then threw herself into his arms, and they hugged each other tightly. Their laughter and screams of joy filled the air and rose into the sky, so that all the stars gathered together to witness their reunion. Hori was hugging her and spinning her around himself cheerfully, while Samatya's feet were no longer touching the earth: she was flying in joy and happiness. Then she burst into tears of disbelief while Hori laughed and reassured her that it was true, not a dream.

Rachel woke up at the sound of the warmth of their meeting, but she stayed inside and smiled as if she was watching them.

Then Samatya whispered to Hori, told him about Rachel, and asked him not to mind her staying with them. Hori smiled and told her that of course he would never mind, as he himself intended to bring her a maid, especially as she would be in her last months of pregnancy.

Samatya's face dropped, and she started to cry once again, but quite differently from a while ago. She distanced herself a little bit from Hori, then informed him that she had been to Malissa as she had felt a severe pain two days earlier, and lost her foetus that night; and as for Rachel, she brought her to be with her as a mother, not as a maid as he said.

Hori's happiness at their reunion changed to shock and sadness after what he'd heard. His dreams were all dashed. How much he had dreamt of having a son accompanying him wherever he went. He had dreamt of having a waggon on which his son would be with him, wandering all over the village. And he had dreamt of throwing him up high in the air, and even of hearing his laughs when he caught him before he fell on the ground. But at that moment, Hori fell from his dreams and onto the ground, sat in silence, and found nothing to say. Samatya sat close to him, and saw his eyes shining wetly; and he turned his face away so as not to be seen like that. She pulled him into her arms as if he was her child. At that moment Hori burst into tears.

After a while, Hori tried to pull himself together and get over what he'd heard. The first thing he said, in a quiet voice, was that he would have to go to Malissa and Samhari in order to thank them for what they had done while he was away. Then he tried to smile and said, "I came back with very good news that I looked forward to telling you about, but …"

"The very good news for me is that you came back safe and sound, and as long as we're together we don't have to think about what happened," Samatya said.

After some time, they went together into the house, and into their room. Samatya told him she would prepare some food for him, but he told her that he had eaten with his companions a while ago on board the boat.

Samatya remembered the big boat that had brought him,

and asked him about it.

"I'll tell you all about it. It's a long and strange story," Hori said while he was changing his clothes.

Then, they got ready for sleep, but they stayed awake till the early hours of next day.

Early that morning, Rachel woke up and went out of the house quietly, sat alone, meditated, and breathed the fresh breezes of the valley.

At that moment, Hori and Samatya fell deep asleep, as they had stayed awake the whole night talking to each other about their news during the time they had been away from each other. Hori told her about what happened to him in the south, and how he was about to lose his life during his attempt to save the chief architect from a certain death.

Also, he told her that the chief architect was a noble man and one of the Pharaoh's relatives. He was so generous with Hori that he had made his private physician treat him till he was completely recovered, and he then chose him to be his personal bodyguard as well.

Then Hori came back with him on his private boat on his way back from the south. When Hori showed him his house, and told him that he was the one who built it himself, the chief architect liked it very much, but when he knew that it was not his own house but was rented, he promised to grant Hori a house of his own, as it was not befitting his personal bodyguard to live in a rented house owned by another man. Even if that man *was* one of the state senior dignitaries, he was still not of the Pharaoh's family.

Eventually, he ordered the boat to be docked for Hori to get off near his house. He also gave him a lot of money, and promised him a big salary as well for his work as a personal bodyguard, that he himself had never dreamed of before.

Little by little, delight returned to Hori's voice while he was recounting to Samatya the details of what had happened to him in the south.

Samatya seemed to be delighted too, but the main reason for her delight, which Hori was completely unaware of, was that they would leave that house forever. But deep in her heart she wished that they could have stayed together peacefully in the same house had she not been through a horrible night there.

Rachel was outside the house. She had tried to make the place clean and tidy: she had moved fallen leaves away from the mat, and rearranged the pillows together side by side. In truth, the place didn't need such an effort, but she liked to leave anywhere she had been looking clean and tidy.

Then, she fell into a deep moment of meditation, and wandered in the realm of God with a heart full of gratitude, which was reflected, and showed clearly, in her eyes. She prayed and thanked God for His great bounty on her, as she was exempted from her previous hard work and her humiliation at that work, and felt her humanity for the first time in her life. At that time, also, she felt the purity of being a slave to her Lord only, rather than the false bondage to the employer.

She started to pray, as she had done for decades, to join her husband and children soon in heaven, but, for the first time, she retreated from that when she remembered Samatya and how generous she was with her. She also remembered her promise to pray to God for her as well.

Then she started to pray.

"O Lord, deprive Samatya not from Your guiding lights. Bestow upon her Your bounties as she was generous with me.

Keep her away from humiliation on the Day of Resurrection as she kept me away from it in this world, O Lord. Deprive her not from the guiding path, and cause me to not die until after I feel reassured about her."

At the same time, Samatya came quietly with the brightness of delight upon her face; then she kissed Rachel's cheek and said, "To whom are you talking, mother?"

Rachel smiled and said, "Talking to my Lord, daughter."

Samatya kissed her once again, and told her that Hori had come back last night. Rachel smiled at her, and told her she knew that as she had been woken up last night by their voices.

Then Samatya said, "As I promised you, I'll make a wonderful lunch today for you, mother."

"Are you sure it is only for me?" Rachel smiled and asked her.

Samatya laughed and said, "Well, it is for both of you, then."

"But I will help you," Rachel said. "I don't like to just sit around like this."

Samatya nodded *yes* and smiled at her.

They had their breakfast both together, while Hori was still asleep. Then they finished cooking lunch together and sat outside the house. It was nearly midday.

As soon as Hori appeared outside the house, Samatya introduced Rachel to him. He greeted her with a quick smile, as if it was just a compliment for Samatya only. Then he told Samatya that he had to go to the chief architect's palace to know his new assignments, and that he would also pass by Malissa's house on his way back to thank her and Samhari.

"Won't you have your breakfast, even?" Samatya said.

He told her that he had already some milk, cheese and

bread; then kissed her and left.

Samatya turned back to Rachel and sat quietly, but she seemed to be worried. Rachel asked her if she was alright as she spotted that worry on her face. Samatya told her that she did not feel reassured because of Hori's new work or his employer as well. Rachel told her that she shouldn't have worried like that, as from her experience in life everything went according to God's will, even if it seemed to us, apparently, that we were the ones who made the choices ourselves.

Hori returned home before sunset. Rachel excused herself and went to her room inside the house to give the couple some privacy together. Samatya prepared food for Hori, and they sat together outside the house. While he was eating he told her about what had happened, and she listened to him. He told her that he had gone to the palace of the chief architect and knew his work assignments. Also, he told her to be prepared as they would move to the new house soon. He conveyed Malissa's regards to Samatya, and told her that he'd met Samhari who'd told him some strange news. "Why didn't you tell me about the representative of the land owner?" he asked.

Samatya sat up, frightened by his unexpected question, and said, "What?"

"What is wrong with you?" Hori asked her back.

She replied calmly to hide her fears, as she noticed that he was now asking about something else. "No, nothing; something just bit me now." Then she tried to add a wondering tone to her voice and said, "What did you say? What happened to him?"

"I know that he disappeared a few days ago, and they are looking for him. Why didn't you tell me?" Hori asked.

Samatya deeply sighed and said, "Yes, I knew that by coincidence when Malissa was here with me, but I didn't know that he is still missing; that's why I forgot about him. But, how did he disappear?"

Hori said, "Samhari told me that all the people in the village are talking about him, but they're all just contradicting each other. They say that his wife informed her neighbour about her husband's multiple relationships with women, then that neighbour disclosed her secret after he disappeared; while some say he was caught together with a woman by her husband, who killed them both. And some say he ran away with one of his lovers. It seems that all are just rumours and nobody knows the truth."

"Oh no, what a weird story!" Samatya said.

Then she said to herself, "How weird those people are. Not one of them thought he might have sought to seduce an unwilling woman, and she killed him defending her honour."

"One day the truth will prevail," Hori said.

"I feel sympathy for his wife. How poor is she, putting up with a lifetime of betrayals—and now his scandals are chasing her after his death," Samatya said spontaneously, without thinking.

"Who told you that he'd died?" Hori asked.

"I don't know; but when a bad man like him disappears, he must be killed for his being the malefactor," Samatya said.

Hori smiled, and said, "My sweetie always has a different point of view, but I can't deny that sometimes I like it, even if I don't agree with it."

Samatya smiled, took a deep breath, got close to him, and said, "And what about the food?"

"Here too, we won't agree with each other," Hori said jokingly, and they both laughed, stood up together, and went inside their house.

CHAPTER X

The New House

The days passed while Hori spent most of his time at work and in preparation for the new house. One morning, they were all prepared to move in, and a luxurious waggon drawn by a horse was waiting outside. It was Hori's private waggon. He and Samatya were busy bringing things that they had decided to take with them and putting them inside the waggon, till they had completely finished.

Eventually, Samatya left the house, tucked her hand under Rachel's arm, and with her other hand carried Rachel's small bundle. They went together to the waggon, got on and waited for Hori. He stood there looking at the house as if he was thinking of something.

"Did you forget something?" Samatya asked.

"No, I'm coming right now," Hori replied, then he came over, got on the waggon, clutched the reins, and got ready to move off.

Samatya repeated her question once again in another form, trying to find out why he'd stood like that. "I thought you had forgotten something inside."

Hori replied in a quiet voice while he was looking towards the house. "No, I didn't forget anything, but I wish I could take the house itself with me. As you know, I got very tired building it; and each piece of stone in its walls, I know its story very well and where it came from."

Samatya patted his back and said, "The whole village knows very well that you are the one who built it, even if it would eventually be lived in later by someone else."

Hori turned and smiled at her, flicked the reins, then the waggon moved off.

While Samatya had different feelings inside her, finally she was released from the nightmare of that house. She sat, excited and delighted, beside Rachel, who shared her happiness by a smile, and patted her hands.

The waggon continued on its way for a considerable distance, and they travelled beyond the boundaries of the local villages. Then the city appeared, with its different and distinctive style of houses. Hori drove the waggon through the streets of the city till they reached a quiet neighborhood. Meanwhile, Samatya's eyes were wide open as if she was watching an impressive art performance on the rhythm of the horse's hooves.

Each house was built distinctively, the colours of the building stones in harmony and consistency with each other in a wonderful architectural design. The houses were detached, and each one of them was surrounded by a fence for privacy. The streets that separated them were wide and paved with stones which were well laid to facilitate the movement of pedestrians and waggons. There were fewer pedestrians, compared to the number of waggons.

The rhythm of the horse's hooves started to slow down till the waggon stopped in front of a gate. Hori smiled and said, "Here is our new house."

Samatya was surprised and said, "Are you serious?"

He laughed and didn't answer, but only beckoned to them

to stay in the waggon. He climbed down quickly, opened the gate, led the horse and the waggon inside, and then closed the gate behind them.

In the meantime, Samatya had already climbed down with Rachel, and was looking at the new place with a smile on her face. It was a wonderful house, but it was clear that it had been unoccupied for a long time. There was a small garden that was in need of a lot of work. They walked together, with Hori in front of them, through the walkway of the garden towards the inner door. They ascended three steps that separated the house from the garden. Hori opened the door and finally they went inside.

The hall was wide, and its walls were covered by soft-white stones. There were many coloured glass windows, beautified by the sun's rays passing through them, that Samatya liked very much. The floor was covered by interconnected turquoise stones, which thrilled Samatya. She hugged Rachel and laughed, as it reminded her of the colour of Rachel's eyes, both colours being so alike.

When they moved a little bit further along, Samatya noticed intermingled coloured light sparkling on the floor. She raised her eyes, and was amazed by the dome that the ceiling was adorned with, and which was made of coloured glass in the same way as the windows which had excited her so much. The pieces of furniture were simple and few: there was just a medium-sized round wooden table surrounded by chairs in the hall.

The house consisted of four rooms, the walls, floors and windows the same colours as the hall. Two rooms were empty, and one of the other two rooms was for Hori and Samatya. It had a big wooden bed furnished with a cotton mattress, a commode on either side of the bed, and a wooden cabinet for clothes. The other room had just a small bed, which was for Rachel. The hall and one room only were furnished with wonderful handmade colourful mats.

After some time, Hori brought their things from the waggon with the help of Samatya. Rachel went to her room and had some rest as she was exhausted from the long trip. Hori explained to Samatya that life in the city was quite different from that in the village. For example, there was a water supplier who, for a payment, would pass by every day to provide people with the water they needed. As for food and other household needs, there was a nearby market to which people went to buy things.

He told her that he had provided the house with enough water, and would bring anything she would need on his way back from work. Also, the kitchen and the bathroom were each separately connected to underground tanks outside the house that were drained from time to time, also for a fee.

Samatya remembered the garden and said, "As for the garden, I will take care of it myself, and one day you'll see how it should be."

Hori laughed and said, "I knew that very well when I saw it the first time. I promise I will take care of it with you, too, when I can. And now, sweetie, I have to go and buy some food."

"You don't have to go, darling," Samatya said. "I brought enough food with me for today and tomorrow as well."

"You always surprise me with nice things," Hori said, smiling. "Let's eat, then, as I'm starving."

Samatya prepared food, then went to Rachel's room, and found her deeply asleep. She closed the door again quietly, went to eat with Hori on the wooden table and sat for the first time in her life on a wooden chair.

The rest of that day passed with arrangements and modifications made by Samatya. As she noticed there was no mat on the floor of Rachel's room, she selected the best one in the hall and put it in there. Also, she brought one commode—the one that belonged to her—from her room and put it beside Rachel's bed.

When Rachel saw that, she said, "Why did you do that, my daughter? I do not need all of this; even the bed itself was too much for me, and I didn't expect this as well."

Samatya hugged her and said, "Don't say that, mother. Everything beautiful that came into my life was because of your blessings. I'm not worthy of all that; I didn't even dream of it."

Round that time, Hori had already gone out and came back late after midnight, while Samatya was fast asleep, and Rachel was in her room.

The next morning, Samatya woke up and didn't find Hori beside her. She got up, frightened, wondering if he'd come back in the night, or he hadn't come back since yesterday. She hurried out of her room to look for him, but didn't find even the waggon outside, so she went back in, went to Rachel's room, knocked on her door and asked her, "Did you see Hori, mother?"

Rachel smiled and said, "Yes, daughter. I woke up late last night to the sound of his waggon, and heard him earlier today going out, too. Don't panic, my daughter, you have to get used to that; it is the nature of his work." Then Samatya was reassured that he was well.

After they had breakfast together, they went out to the

garden. Samatya's eyes were full of enthusiasm, wandering all over the garden as if she was planning how to restore its life. Rachel noticed that, and helped her in removing unnecessary weeds and stones from its soil.

Samatya turned the soil over with a hoe, aerated and exposed it to the sun, and divided the garden into sections, as if she was following a precise map in her mind.

They spent quite some time on this tough job, but Samatya did not mind that. Then they heard a knocking on the gate. Samatya got scared and grabbed Rachel's arm.

Rachel patted her hand and said, "Calm down, daughter. I'll see for myself who is there." She went towards the gate, and opened its small window to check who was there. It was the water supplier. He greeted her, and told her that his master Hori had enjoined him to pass by from time to time to see if they were in need of water.

Samatya heard what he said, but couldn't see him. She beckoned to Rachel to indicate that they didn't need any at that moment and that it might be the next day or later. Rachel told him what Samatya said, talked to him for a while, and then closed the small window, all the time smiling.

"What's the matter?" Samatya asked.

"He is a young man called Benjamin, from my village. He knew me but I didn't know him. He said that he'd known me since he was a child," Rachel replied.

Samatya smiled and said, "Didn't you see? He will take much better care of us now, also because of you, not because of Hori."

Rachel smiled and felt reassured about this young man, but didn't know why.

Hori came back from work and had his lunch. He talked

about work all the time, and Samatya listened. After he had finished talking, Samatya asked him to buy her some seeds for the garden if possible.

He paused for a moment and said, "Well, I have to buy everything the house needs. Do I have to buy seeds as well."

Samatya felt that he was upset because he had too many burdens to bear, so she said, "You don't have to, darling, I will go to the market myself with Rachel, tomorrow. It will be a good opportunity to see the city and the market, and to buy all that we need, and the seeds as well."

"How will you get there?" Hori asked.

"Don't worry, we will ask someone," Samatya replied.

"Well, anyway, the market is nearby, but take care. Life here is different from the village. Just don't talk to any strangers, get your things, and come back home soon," Hori said.

Samatya smiled and said, "Don't worry, darling."

CHAPTER XI

The City Market

The next morning, Samatya woke up, and again found that Hori wasn't beside her. This time she didn't worry as she had before. She was reassured, with a bright smile upon her face, that she would go out with Rachel to the market.

Then she quickly had her breakfast with Rachel, and they prepared to go out. They stood in front of the house and looked right and left, but didn't know which direction to go. They stayed where they were for some time, waiting for a waggon to take them where they wanted to go, or somebody that they might ask, but neither of these happened.

"Let's go this way, mother. We must find someone to ask," Samatya said.

They walked along together. It was still early in the morning, so there was no one on the street, especially as it was a quiet neighbourhood. They kept walking from one street to another, and finally found a main street a little further away. It seemed to be a little crowded. They walked faster, enthusiastically, then Samatya stopped a waggon and said to the waggoner, "We want to go to the city market." He beckoned to them to get on, and then moved off.

On their way, they kept watching life along the city streets. After quite some time, Samatya felt worried as they were some considerable distance from home, although Hori had told her that the market was nearby.

"Where is the market?" Samatya asked the waggoner.

"We are about to arrive, madam," he said. "Don't you know where the market is?"

She didn't answer him back, and pretended to be busy talking to Rachel, as she remembered Hori's words not to talk to strangers.

After a while the waggon stopped, and Samatya knew that they arrived at the market, as she'd spotted its big gate. It seemed to her as if it was a big festival, not a place to buy and sell. She hadn't expected it to be so spectacular.

Samatya gave the fare to the waggoner, while he tried to start a conversation with her, and said, "If waggons were allowed through the gate, I would accompany you around inside, madam."

Samatya didn't like the way he looked at her, so she didn't pay any attention, got off the waggon with Rachel, and they walked together towards the market. He called to her and said, "Madam, would you like me to wait for you?" Although she heard him very well, she didn't even look back.

Rachel whispered to Samatya, and said, "I liked your attitude towards that waggoner, daughter. A woman is the one who really has the reins that direct a relationship with any man. If she only spoke softly, she would make any sick-minded man think evil thoughts about her."

Samatya remembered what happened to her that horrific night, thought that she might have caused the representative of the landowner to think evil about her by talking innocently to him before, although he was also a sick-minded person. Then, she sighed and said, "Yes, it's true, mother, it's true."

Then they went on much further, and melted into the

crowd. They could hardly hear each other because of the immense amount of noise there; and sometimes they couldn't hear each other at all.

Samatya hadn't imagined the market to be so huge. It was a city inside the city itself: streets, roads, and people queuing up to buy what they needed, as if those goods would run out and not be available tomorrow.

There was nothing you could think of that wasn't available there as long as one had the money to pay for it. The way the fruits and vegetables were displayed caught Samatya's eye, as if she was seeing them for the first time in her life. They were overlapped together in an artistic way that caught the attention of passers-by.

A long time passed while they were wandering all over the market, as if they had forgotten the reason why they had gone there.

Samatya looked around, and began to buy what she needed. Eventually they both got tired because they were overloaded with the weight of everything they'd bought. Suddenly, they stopped, and couldn't go any further. At that moment, a young boy with a pushcart appeared and offered his services for a fee. They both put everything that they had into the pushcart, and the young boy accompanied them wherever they went.

Samatya bought everything she needed but the seeds. She stopped by one of the vendors who had all kinds of plants and flowers on display. There was a large crowd of people there. Some were asking about the prices, some were ordering what they needed, some were pushing the vendor to respond to them, and other things too, while Rachel and the young boy were waiting to catch his eye.

No sooner had the vendor spotted Samatya among the

crowd than he paid her full attention, and asked her what she needed. People got angry because it was clear that he was giving her priority above all of them, but he didn't care about that. Samatya took the seeds, paid for them, and left while people were still looking at her; some of them in admiration, especially men; and some others with indignation, especially women.

Then, Samatya and Rachel burst out laughing together.

"What logic that man adopts in dealing with his customers," Rachel said. "He would lose them all just to please you. What did he gain then?"

Samatya laughed and said, "I really wonder why some of those men are acting like that."

All the while the young boy was following what they said, but didn't understand anything. "We want to go back to the market gate, please," Samatya said to him.

"Which one do you want?" he asked. "There are many of them."

Samatya replied confidently, "Any gate. It does not matter. Just take us there so that we can get a waggon"

The boy beckoned to them to follow him. After quite a distance, they reached where they were going. Samatya beckoned to a waggon to stop, and the young boy unloaded his pushcart into it. Samatya paid the young boy generously; he thanked her and rushed back towards the market cheerfully.

"We want to get to Hori's house," Samatya said to the waggoner after she had got on with Rachel.

"Hori's house? Where is that, madam?" the waggoner asked her in a wondering tone.

"Hori, the personal bodyguard of the chief architect," she replied confidently.

"Madam, who is Hori, and who is the chief architect?" the waggoner asked.

"Oh, son, we don't know where the house is," Rachel said. "All we know is that the owner of that house is the personal bodyguard of the chief architect, who is a relative of the Pharaoh."

The waggoner got frightened upon hearing the name of the Pharaoh, and said in a humble tone, "Glory be to the Pharaoh. But, madam, there are a lot of architects who are relatives of the great Pharaoh, and even if I knew that architect, I could never dare to go to his house and ask about his bodyguard address. He would cut off my head there and then."

At that point, Rachel knew, and deep down so did Samatya, that they were lost together in the city.

Hori came back home from his work to find only silence. He entered his room but didn't find Samatya there; then he looked for her everywhere but he found neither her nor Rachel.

He was owned by his fear, and said to himself, "Where can they be? Is it possible to stay this late in the market?"

He rushed quickly outside and went to the nearby market. He looked for them everywhere there, but uselessly, while the crowd there seemed to melt away. He asked the vendors about them, but no one had an answer. He also asked if anything unusual had happened there on that day, but he was told that everything was quite normal. Hori got very worried. He wandered through all the streets around the house till he was somewhat further away, and then came back, restarting over and over, uselessly.

He came back to the house once again, but they were still not there. Then he had an idea. He hurried outside, and reported them as missing to the soldiers of the interior security of the city.

At that point, Samatya and Rachel had still not moved from where they were, not knowing how to get home. Samatya was scared that they would be lost forever, and if they *could* return home, she was scared too of Hori's anger that they had come back so late. Then people started to gather round them, and tried to help, but no one could do anything.

Samatya felt as if she was choking, and remembered a similar moment during that hard night when she was helpless and unable to do anything. Once again, but in silence, without even moving her lips, she prayed to the real God. "Oh God, my real God, oh You who created me, guide us back home, and do not let Hori be angry with me."

At the same time, Rachel raised her eyes up to the sky, while Samatya, afraid, grasped hold of her.

All at once, from amongst the crowd around them, someone appeared, curious to find out what was going on. Suddenly, he said in a loud voice, "Mother, what is the matter with you?"

It was Benjamin, the water supplier. Rachel told him what had happened.

"Don't panic, mother, I know the way very well," he said. Then, he brought a waggon for them. They got on; he put all their things quickly in the waggon; and sat beside the driver and they all moved off.

At the same time, the soldiers from interior security were searching for them everywhere.

Eventually, Samatya and Rachel returned home safely. Samatya was crying, and said, "I can't believe what happened to us. I didn't think we'd ever get back here again. I can't believe how we finally came back home so easily."

Rachel said, "I prayed to God, and I was quite sure He would respond to me, so I wasn't surprised that we got back here, but I wonder how to thank Him as befits the Glory of His face and the greatness of His might."

Samatya didn't concentrate on what Rachel was saying as she was busy thinking of Hori and what he would do if he had already come back home and not found them.

Night came and threw its black cloak over the city. Hori was still out looking for them, overwhelmed by despair that he wouldn't find Samatya again. Something bad must have happened to her, he thought. He tried to drive the thought from his mind, but it came back and attacked him again and again.

He returned home helplessly, with little hope that he might find her. But no sooner had Samatya heard the gate open than she shrank back in fear, while Hori rushed towards her as if he himself was a lost child that had eventually found its mother, and hugged her.

Ambiguous events often become clear after they are over. Samatya now knew that Hori hadn't meant the city market itself, but the nearby one. He also knew that he had made a mistake by leaving her to go out to a place that she has never been to before. Anyway, the bitterness of the bad experience had gone, and sweetness of the adventure in the city market remained.

The next day, Samatya was in her room alone thinking of the previous day's adventure with a smile on her face. She was still impressed by that big market. Then, she remembered her prayer yesterday, that she hadn't even moved her lips. She linked that to what Rachel had said before about how our hearts would grasp God. She felt chills all over her body. She faced herself frankly and said, "Was it a coincidence that my prayer on that hard night came true, and I was saved from that disaster? Was it a coincidence, too, that my prayer of yesterday also came true and we got back home safely? Was it a coincidence that my fears about Hori yesterday were replaced by his fears for myself? Was it a coincidence that Rachel came into my life and I learned from her what she said about her God? Surely, the real God who I prayed to in the old house and who I prayed to yesterday was Himself the God that Rachel told me about. And, all that happened to me, and all that I felt, was exactly as same as Rachel described to me about her God." She continued with her deep thoughts and added, "The real God neither lets his slave down nor overlooks him. He must respond to his prayers in hard times even if they were only by his heart, whenever and wherever. He must not be the sun, He must not be a human being as well. Then the real God that I was looking for is the same God of Rachel. Yes, He is my God."

The tears coursed down her face.

When Hori came back from work and saw her tears, he patted her hands and told her to forget what had happened the day before. He had himself forgotten everything. The most important thing was that she had come back safely, and he was unable to describe his happiness about that.

Samatya threw herself into his arms and wept hard. His words undoubtedly had a touching effect upon her, but the main reason for her tears was, as she said to herself, "And I can't describe my happiness that I found God." Then she retreated and said, "But, it was God who found me when I was lost on my way looking for Him."

Samatya's tears never stopped, but increased, while she was still in Hori's arms.

"Sweetie, calm down, please," Hori said. "It was my own fault. I had to buy what you asked for myself." Then he smiled and said, "Listen, my dear, I will make it up to you. I will reward you with something you have never dreamed of before."

But nothing he said changed the way she felt.

He resumed, and said, "I will take you with me to a big festival. It will be more beautiful than what you saw in the city market itself. Here in the city, as I've been told, the Festival Day is quite different from any other place. I'm quite sure that Festival Day will be a great event for you."

Samatya smiled at him by way of thanks, but what she felt inside her heart would never end. It seemed to be just a start.

CHAPTER XII

Preparation for the Festival

A new day was brightened by a sun that seemed quite different from yesterday's; or so it seemed to Samatya's eyes, and as felt by her heart also. Her face looked brighter and more beautiful as well.

The day before, Samatya had surprised Rachel, and told her that she believed in God. Rachel was very pleased, fell down prostrate, and thanked God that He had responded to her prayers. She also told Samatya that Malissa had done the same as her a long time ago, but was hiding her faith. Because of this, Samatya now understood the secret behind the sadness and bewilderment of Malissa during that night they'd spent together.

Then, Samatya felt such an urge to see Malissa that she asked Hori if she could visit her with Rachel.

"Why don't you wait till the day of the festival, and she'll come to celebrate with us here with Samhari and their children too?" Hori said.

As if he had inspired her with the idea, she said, "Well, why don't you tell Samhari to bring her with the children to stay with me till the day of the festival, then they can all go home together?"

"I'll do that, but I hope he agrees," Hori said, and then went out to work.

Samatya resumed her work in the garden, planted the seeds in the soil and irrigated it, with some help from Rachel while they were talking together.

Samatya's thirst to know more from Rachel was like the thirst of that abandoned soil for water. Rachel told her all that she knew to quench her thirst, just as the water quenched the soil's.

After Samatya had finished what she was doing, she sighed and said, "I'm impatient to see this plant grow, mother. I would like to see it become a lush garden."

"You prepared its soil very well, selected the finest seeds, and you had all the means to make it a lush garden, so God won't waste your good effort by His will, daughter."

The same evening, Hori came back home from work and brought some good news for Samatya: that he had met one of Samhari's neighbours earlier that day, asked him to tell Samhari about Samatya's suggestion, and described their house location to him too.

The next day passed sluggishly, as Samatya was expecting Malissa to come, but it seemed to her that Samhari didn't agree, and she felt disappointed. Rachel told her that Malissa and her husband might be busy in their work, or that the neighbour had forgotten to pass Hori's message on.

Samatya asked Rachel to recount to her all the stories of prophets that she knew. She listened to Rachel while her eyes were fixed staring at the soil, as if she was expecting to see her plants break ground there and then.

After quite some time, Hori came back home loaded with a lot of things. Rachel quietly headed inside to her room. Samatya helped Hori carry some of those things into their room together. He surprised her with new clothes and gold jewellery for her. She was very pleased, and said, "What about you, darling?"

"Of course I didn't forget to buy new clothes for me too for Festival Day, sweetie."

Samatya smiled, but her smile faded and almost disappeared. Hori looked at her and said, "I bought new clothes for Rachel too. After all, it is Festival Day."

Samatya was delighted, hugged and thanked him, although she knew that he'd bought Rachel new clothes just to improve his appearance on the day.

After a while, Samatya put on some of her new clothes and a few items of the jewellery. Hori was amazed and said, "Oh, you look stunning, sweetie. If it was up to me, I would have you crowned queen and put you on the throne."

"And you would become the Pharaoh, then?" Samatya said, laughing out loud and teasing him. He tried to pretend that he was angry at what she'd said; but he failed, and burst out laughing with her too.

Then, she took Rachel's new clothes and went to her room. "Hori bought this gift for you, mother," she said.

"God bless him. Please thank him for me, my daughter," Rachel smiled and said.

Then Samatya put a gold necklace around her neck and said, "And this is my gift for you, mother."

Rachel hugged Samatya and said, "You are my gift, my dear daughter; but I never wear gold."

"Is it forbidden, mother?" Samatya asked.

"No, daughter, it is not, but I don't wear it," Rachel replied sadly.

Samatya supposed that gold did not suit Rachel after her tragedy, so she quickly tried to amend the situation and pulled her arm and said, "Come on, mother, you can thank Hori yourself."

They went out of Rachel's room in a hurry, and were surprised by Hori who was in front of them.

"My mother wanted to thank you, Hori, for the gift," Samatya said.

Hori noticed a deep sadness inside Rachel's eyes that touched his heart. It was the very first time their eyes had actually met. He smiled at her.

"Thank you, son, for your gift and your concern," Rachel said in a quiet voice. "I would like to thank you, also, for your generosity in welcoming me into your house."

Hori addressed Rachel with a smile on his face while he was looking at Samatya: "Samatya likes you immensely, and I always trust her opinion, so whoever she likes that much is surely worthy of it."

Samatya and Rachel were surprised to hear him speak thus. He himself didn't know how he had been able to say it. It was as if it wasn't him speaking.

CHAPTER XIII

News from the Royal Palace

The next morning, Hori went to his work as usual. Samatya spent her time with Rachel preparing food, and continued their never-ending conversations. Suddenly, they heard a knocking on the house gate. They went together to see who was there and found that it was Malissa.

Samatya hurriedly opened the gate, feeling happy. It was a warm and loud reunion that brought the three friends all together once again. No sooner had Malissa known that Samatya had become a believer than she yelled with joy, hugged and congratulated her, all the while crying. They were both excited, their conversation was loud and full of enthusiasm, while Rachel was quieter, but glad and contented. They were all talking at the same time, each one wanting to tell the others their news. Samatya was asking Malissa about her children and why she hadn't brought them with her; Rachel was asking her whether she had got to the house easily; while Malissa continued something she had started to say, and tried to answer them both at the same time.

She told them that she had come directly from her work as it was rather nearer than her house; her children would come later with Samhari. And she had brought her clothes and everything she would need for the Festival.

Suddenly, she remembered and congratulated Samatya on

the new house, then she told them that she missed them so much.

"Come on, Malissa, change your clothes while I bring some food so that we can have lunch together," Samatya said.

"I finally managed to convince Samhari to allow me to come alone," Malissa said.

Thus, their conversation continued for quite some time, loudly and randomly. All at once, Malissa beckoned to them both with her hands to stop talking and whispered to them.

"Did you know what happened in the Pharaoh's palace?"

They wondered together. "What happened?"

Malissa looked round and started to speak with a lower voice. Samatya interrupted her, pulled them both and said, "Let's go inside."

They all went together into the house and sat at the round table in the hall.

"Oh my God," said Malissa. "The house is so beautiful. The colour of the floor is amazing, Samatya."

"Thank you, darling," Samatya said, smiling, but soon she changed her tone of voice and said. "There is no time now for that, Malissa. Come on, tell us what happened."

"Some news has spread among the workers inside the palace I work in. One of the guards who works in the Pharaoh's main palace told his mistress who works with us as a supervisor, then she told her friend who works with us in the kitchen as a cook, then the news … "

Samatya impatiently interrupted her and said, "Malissa, spit it out, please, without introductions."

Rachel burst out laughing because of Samatya's impatience and Malissa's narration of the fine details. Malissa and Samatya shared her laughter too.

"A man from the Children of Israel came to the Pharaoh's palace. He told the Pharaoh that he was a prophet sent by God to him. He denied that the Pharaoh was a god too. The Pharaoh got angry and said, 'You are a madman and a liar'.

"Then, that man's staff turned into a big snake. The Pharaoh said to him, 'You are a magician', and threatened to kill the man as well," Malissa said.

Samatya looked at Rachel as if she wanted her to explain what she had heard from Malissa.

"Who *is* that man?" Rachel asked.

"They say that he is Prince Moses, who was brought up in the Pharaoh's palace and ran away after he killed an Egyptian man many years ago," Malissa replied.

"Do you know him, mother?" Samatya asked.

"I don't know him personally, but I heard about him many years ago. He is one of my people, despite the fact that he was brought up inside the Pharaoh's palace, and is considered to be one of the Pharaoh's family, but he has a good reputation, and is quite different from the rest of them," Rachel replied.

"Carry on, Malissa. What happened then?" Samatya asked.

"They say that the Pharaoh was about to kill him, but Haman and his other counsellors advised him to put it off for a while. That's all that they say," Malissa replied.

"Mother, do you think, he is himself the prophet whose time is coming?" Samatya asked.

Rachel kept silent for a while, and then said, "I cannot say either way, daughter."

"But Malissa said that his staff turned into a big snake. Could it be his miracle?" Samatya asked.

"It is very confusing. Magicians can change anything into something else. Should we believe that each magician is a prophet, and his magic is a miracle, then?" Malissa said. Rachel did not answer.

"Yes, you're right, Malissa. I think he is not a prophet," Samatya said.

"We can't confirm, daughters, if he is a magician or a prophet," Rachel said.

"Who *can* confirm, then, mother?" Malissa asked.

"Let's think about it," Rachel replied.

"I will prepare lunch, and then we will find a solution, by God's will," Samatya said.

Malissa smiled and hugged Samatya when she said, "By God's will."

"I'm so happy, dear, to hear you say that," Malissa said.

"Thank God for His grace, Malissa," Samatya said.

Then they prepared lunch together, sat round the table, and started to eat in silence. They were thinking very hard about that confusing riddle. Rachel broke the silence, saying, "I will ask you a question. Suppose that I have a piece of jewellery, you don't know me at all, and I tell you it is made of pure gold and I want to sell it to you. How could you know if it is genuine or not?"

Malissa quickly replied, "We go to a trustworthy gold dealer and ask him."

"Exactly. That's what I mean," Rachel said.

"Did you mean, mother, that the one who can judge if he was a prophet or magician is a magician too?" Samatya asked.

"That's it, but not any magician. He must be a trustworthy one," Rachel replied.

"But, that trustworthy magician may claim, for some reason, that the man is not a prophet," Samatya said.

"Each prophet, my daughter, has enemies who plot against

him for sure, but by the end, God will make the truth prevail," Rachel said.

Samatya seemed to be bewildered and said, "I thought it would be much easier, but it is very complicated. I would have thought the prophet's miracle would be quite enough for people to make them believe."

"If what we heard is true, it is meant to be this complicated, Samatya, as it is a test and trial for people," Malissa said. "No one will believe other than those who have minds to understand the truth. And, as mother said, the truth will prevail. Also, I think that such news as we heard is not enough to judge whether that man is a prophet or not—and perhaps all that we heard are just rumours."

CHAPTER XIV

The Buds of the Garden

The three friends spent most of their time together talking about what had happened inside the Pharaoh's palace. In the evening, Samatya stayed with them in Rachel's room till late, then she went to sleep in her room. Malissa and Rachel decided to sleep on the floor together and sacrifice the small bed that was not wide enough for two.

The next day, Samatya woke up early and had breakfast with Hori, while the other two friends were still asleep.

"Your idea to bring Malissa here was quite right. This way I'm reassured that Samhari will attend the festival tomorrow," Hori said.

"What is your point about Samhari attending the festival tomorrow?" Samatya asked.

"I will be reassured, sweetie, that he will accompany you all, as I will be busy tomorrow all day long with the chief architect," Hori replied.

"I thought he would let you spend the Festival Day with your family," Samatya said in a sad, quiet tone.

Hori tried to make it easier for her, and said, "Sweetie, I forgot to tell you, and you were busy with your friends too. Yesterday, I found out that a royal decree will be proclaimed today over all the lands, that all people have to attend the big celebration of the Festival Day held in the Royal Celebration

Arena. The great Pharaoh will attend it himself, and all the senior officials. It is clear that it will be a big, sensitive occasion, and I have to accompany the chief architect all the time."

Samatya asked in a wondering tone, "Is it normal for the Pharaoh to issue a royal decree to make people celebrate the Festival Day?"

He replied in a hurry, as if he was hiding something, gave no importance to her question, and said, "Anyway, tomorrow is close, if you wait for it."

Then, Samatya saw him off at the gate, and he went to work. She sat next to her plants and thought about what Hori had told her. She was quite sure that what he said had something to do with what Malissa had said the day before. Then she smiled when she spotted little buds trying to come out of the soil. After a while, Rachel came out and greeted Samatya. She smiled, too, when she spotted the little buds.

Samatya told her about what she had heard from Hori, and what she had concluded as well, then she asked her for her opinion.

"If your conclusion is right, daughter, it would be a sign that someone is plotting something big," Rachel said.

"I almost get what you mean, mother, but explain it to me some more, please," Samatya said.

"If that man was not a prophet, but just a magician, why would the Pharaoh gather people together, then?" Rachel said. "Is it to warn them? I don't think so. Then, the Pharaoh must be quite sure that he is truly a prophet, and this is surely a plot against that man."

"If that man was truly a prophet, as you said, the Pharaoh would have killed him at once," Samatya said.

"I coudn't confirm it yet, daughter, but the Pharaoh would

not have killed him—contrary to what you said—if he was a true prophet, as the Pharaoh is more cunning than this. If he killed the man, he would prove his prophethood, so I tend more to think that the Pharaoh is plotting to make him ruin his image in front of people so they won't listen to him later, and just mock him."

Samatya didn't seem to share her opinion and said, "It's confusing, mother. Anyway, hearts have a major role to play here, and tomorrow we will see."

Malissa came out and greeted them and said, "You're still talking about the same thing, aren't you?"

Samatya laughed, got up, and said, "I will prepare breakfast for you to have here in the garden, and then we can continue our talk. What do you think?" Then, she went inside alone, and told them to stay.

While Samatya was inside, Rachel told Malissa about the news that Samatya had heard from Hori.

"I agree with you, mother, but I must add something else," Malissa replied. "The Pharaoh can't kill that man as he is one of the Children of Israel; and as you know, there are a lot of them who work inside his palaces, on his land, and all over the country. He is not so stupid as to ruin a system inside his kingdom. Of course, he could kill him and all the Children of Israel easily if he wanted, but what prevents him is the benefit, and the more important thing that if he *did* kill that man, he would prove that he *is* a true prophet. Thus his image as a so-called god in front of his people would be shaken, and this is more important to him than the benefit of all the lands.

"Tomorrow, the truth will appear. You forgot something very important: that we have never seen this man before. When we do see him, it will be much easier for us to judge him."

After some time, Samatya came back with food, while Rachel and Malissa prepared a place, furnished a mat, and then waited for her. Suddenly they panicked, hearing quick, hard knocking on the gate. It was clear there was more than one person out there, but then they all laughed together when they heard Malissa's children calling their mother, and Samhari asking them to stop it and keep quiet.

Malissa opened up, and they rushed quickly into the house and hugged their mother. Samhari was in a hurry and told her that he had to go and would be back tomorrow to take them all to the Festival. He greeted Samatya when he saw her, and left quickly.

The three young boys filled the whole house with noise and joy. Each one of them was showing his new clothes and toys to his mother. Malissa asked them to be polite and to keep quiet, but to no avail.

When Hori returned from work, the young boys got very excited at seeing the horse and the waggon in the garden. Hori welcomed them and said, "I will have my lunch first, and then take you all for a ride in the waggon. Would you like that?"

The boys were very pleased, and clapped their hands. They all climbed into the waggon, sat together side by side and waited for Hori.

After Hori had finished his lunch, he took them out as he had promised, and Samatya saw them off, smiling. No sooner had the waggon passed through the gate on its way out than their loud voices faded out little by little till they were absolutely quiet once again.

In the evening, Hori came back with the children, who were excited and happy. They told their mother where they'd gone to and what Hori had bought for them. Soon they calmed down and fell into a quiet, deep sleep; then so did Malissa, and then Rachel, last of all.

Meanwhile, Hori and Samatya sat together on the mat in the garden till the early hours of the next day. Each one of them was reading the other's mind through their eyes, but Samatya's tears disclosed it to Hori. He embraced her, smiled, and said, "My sweetie and beloved, it is neither in your hands nor in mine. My darling, one day we will have many children, and you will remember that; and we will have a big palace by the river, with a wide garden that they will be able to play in. And we will be both sitting together like now, watching them while they play and run around us."

CHAPTER XV

The Festival Day

The dawn light brightened, as if it were a bringer of good news to those who were still alive and awake since the previous night, so that they could witness the Festival Day; and a warning to those still fast asleep to wake up willingly, or be woken unwillingly by a blast on the feast trumpet.

Samatya's eyes were still wide open since last night, while Hori was still asleep, his head in her lap, after a long conversation between them that had lasted all night long in the garden.

Sounds of laughter, shouts of joy, music, rhythm, and collective chants were all blending together quietly from, it seemed to Samatya's ears, a faraway place. Suddenly, those sounds grew louder, and then started to fade out little by little, returning again to ripple quietly again and again like waves on the sea.

A trumpet blast rode one of those waves; it was just one of Malissa's children announcing the coming of the feast, in his own way, from Rachel's room. Hori woke up in panic, while Samatya laughed out loud and said, "Happy feast day, Hori. May you always be my beloved, each and every year."

He smiled and hugged her, wished her the same too, then got up hurriedly and said, "I have to go right now. I'll leave the waggon as I won't need it. Samhari could take it as he won't easily find one today to take you to the Festival." Then, he rushed to their room to change his clothes.

While Samatya was on her way to the kitchen to prepare breakfast, she heard Malissa inside the room, whispering sharply, rebuking her child for something he'd done. "Let them be, Malissa," she said. "It *is* the feast day, darling."

It seemed that the children must have heard Samatya very well: they obeyed her at once. The door opened, and all of them rushed quickly outside to the garden and gathered round the horse, pleased to see it. It seemed to be pleased with their company too.

Hori had his breakfast quickly and went out in a hurry, greeting the children and wishing them well for the feast, and left. Rachel and Malissa came out of their room and greeted Samatya as well. Samatya told them that they had to have their breakfast quickly, prepare some food to take with them for the children, and to get ready before Samhari arrived.

After a while they were all ready, wearing their new clothes, and they looked cheerful and elegant as befitted that cheerful day. Samatya's delight in being a believer was her 'real' new dress for that feast, rather than simply the new clothes that she was wearing.

Samhari came on time and took them all in the waggon as Hori had suggested. The children rushed to sit side by side in the front of the waggon beside their father, with the three friends sitting in the back together. Then they moved off. The rhythm of the horse's footsteps grew less and less till it vanished among the sounds of celebrations that filled all the city.

All of them were impressed by the roads and the streets which were decorated with colourful banners and flags, as if they were wearing their new clothes to celebrate the feast, too. Also, they were jammed with old and young passers-by in brightly coloured clothes, who flowed together in big crowds as if they were a field of moving flowers, or a live painting.

Those big crowds increased little by little, and headed towards one destination, which was the Royal Celebration Arena. The waggon got so slowed down because of the crowds that the footsteps of the passers-by were faster than those of the horse himself. It was a good opportunity for those inside the waggon to watch that live painting closely, but the slow progress made the distance seem much longer.

Then they saw sailboats, swaying gracefully, celebrating in their own way on the river, as if they and the flood were the river's gift to the feast. And shouts of joy overshadowed the sound of music bands that spread everywhere.

The crowds continued crawling in from everywhere, and got closer, little by little, to the Celebration Arena, where the soldiers were highly organised and lined up on both sides as if preparing for a battle that would determine their fate.

The waggon had to stop a little far away from the Celebration Arena. It was not allowed to go any further, as there was a dedicated parking place for waggons. All of them got off; Samatya held Rachel's hand, Malissa held the hand of one of her children, and Samhari was behind them between the two other children, holding their hands. They kept walking for quite a distance among hordes of people heading towards one of the entry gates.

No sooner had they passed through the gate than they were stunned by the splendour of the enormous, sumptuous flowers with which the arena had been decorated, that not only superseded the number of people themselves, but also overshadowed the colours of their clothes. The wonderful fragrance permeated the place, as if one of Heaven's doors was about to be opened.

Everything there was prepared and carried out perfectly as befitted such a royal ceremony attended by the Pharaoh himself. The golden colour was the dominant one among all other colours throughout the arena, in the Royal Box, on the statues, and the ornaments of women, children and men, that shimmered in the sunlight that increased its brilliance and glamour. The grand statues of the Pharaoh towered above everything, staring at people and terrorising them, so they lowered their eyelids in servility, enjoying that bondage they had invented for themselves, as it was they who had created their Pharaoh. Meanwhile, the soldiers spread everywhere, organising the crowds, and also providing security.

Inside, the arena was huge, surrounded by circular terraces which were full to bursting because of the huge numbers in the audience. At the same time, the Royal Box was still empty, waiting for more to come. The crowd overflowed around the yard to the extent that the soldiers had to urge them to move back to make room for the show.

The audience started to calm down, and all were settled in their places. The noise calmed down, too, so that the sound of music, that had never stopped, could finally be heard.

They were so lucky that they had managed to get a place in the terraces that was close to the performance area. But it was so crowded that Samhari took two of his children on his lap, while Malissa sat next to him and took the third one on *her* lap. On her other side, Samatya sat with Rachel next to her. It was clear that those terraces were holding many more than they were supposed to, as if they were gathered together on the Day of Resurrection.

After quite some time, blasts from the royal trumpets echoed all over the arena, followed by the caller's voice, which announced, "The great god Pharaoh's procession."

All corners of the arena were shaken by the repeated echoing shouts: "Long live the god Pharaoh."

No sooner had the Royal carriage entered, surrounded by the war chariots and soldiers, than the whole audience stood up together, and clapped with nonstop thundering shouts and cheers; so much so that Malissa's children got frightened and kept screaming. The three friends were busy trying to calm them down, while not forgetting to hail the Pharaoh their own way, saying, "Woe to you."

The Pharaoh got down from his royal carriage and, headed by his entourage and soldiers, walked steadily, haughtily and slowly, delighted by the shouts and cheers that were being showered upon him, like a roaring cascade in a deep and far-off place inside the hell of himself which could never be sated. Then, he roused them further by pointing his mace at them on his way to the Royal Box, so they increased their cheers and shouts as if they were to never run out.

Then, other processions came on, one by one, carrying the Pharaoh's wives, daughters and sons, and all the other members of his family, till all were settled in their places. The sounds of cheers and shouts didn't stop till the royal trumpets were blown once again; then, the whole arena fell silent.

The callers announced that it was time for the Pharaoh's speech; and all were eager to know what he would say. The Pharaoh started his speech, after which the callers repeated what he had said to convey his speech to everyone in the arena.

"O, people of Egypt, we have gathered you all here on the Day of the Festival—your feast—on which the River Nile is flowing with bounties upon you all, and upon all the land of Egypt.

"This is our gift, which we have bestowed upon you all. We have not deprived you of it even for one day; and how could we deprive you when we know well that you have no god but me? Have you ever known that you had any god other than me?"

The whole audience, as with one voice, shouted, "Long live the god Pharaoh." They kept repeating their hails till the trumpets were blown again, when once more they all kept silent.

The Pharaoh resumed his speech.

"O people of Egypt, we gathered you here today to show you that which only we see, to show you what threatens you. Surely we have saved you before from many other threats, and how could we save you were I not your lord most high?

"O people of Egypt, the danger that has come today to threaten you, to deprive you of your bounties, to dissuade you from worshipping your beloved god, and to remove you from your lands, did not come from outside your lands as you might expect—but from amongst you.

"He was brought up amongst you as a child, ate from the bounties of your lands. He came today to thank you by calling you disbelievers, and to corrupt your religion and your life too.

"It is Moses who did not appreciate our grace upon him, but denied it. He learned magic and claimed to be a prophet. We did not kill him, though we were able to do so, but were merciful towards him as it seemed that he had lost his mind, just as we were merciful towards him before, when he was brought to us as a child with no mind.

"Then, after he had grown to full strength amongst you, he came with the magic that he had learned, after which he ran away after he had killed one of you, that all of you know very well. Now he returned, with his magic and the so-called prophethood.

"So, we appointed a meeting today for him to come along with his magic. We also brought him our well-versed and trustworthy magicians to discredit his magic in front of you all, and to prove before your eyes that he is a liar, and not a prophet as he claimed to be. He claimed that he was sent by his god to you, while we sent no prophets to you. Why would we send you prophets, while I myself, your god, am here amongst you?

"O people of Egypt, we gathered you here today to witness his lies with your own eyes. Here am I, your lord, who shows you only that which he sees. So, does anyone here see something other than what I see?"

The audience kept silent for a while. They seemed shocked by what they had heard, so one of the Pharaoh's entourage cried out loud to stimulate them.

"Moses is a magician."

"Long live the god Pharaoh."

Then, all of them echoed what they heard without thinking, as they had done for decades: that they devoted themselves in bondage to their Pharaoh.

Once again, the trumpets blasts stopped their shouts and cheers; then the callers announced the entry into the arena of the Pharaoh's magicians. A large number of magicians entered, bowed to the Pharaoh, then lined up together and waited with eyes shining with challenge.

Then, the callers announced the entry of Moses, and Aaron, his brother. The audience started humming, winked one to another in mockery and laughed, while Moses and his brother Aaron (Peace Be Upon Them Both) entered quietly and steadily in peace.

It was quite clear to the audience that Moses talked angrily with the magicians, but no one heard what they said to each other, while the magicians seemed to talk to him in challenge and mockery as well.

At that moment, Samatya and Rachel looked at each other while Rachel held Samatya's hand, and they resumed watching to see what would happen next.

Then, the magicians started to throw their ropes and staffs to the ground, and cried out loud, "By the might of Pharaoh, it is we who will certainly win."[1]

Their ropes and staffs appeared to become snakes by magic. To all people, even to Moses himself, they seemed to move fast. The whole arena was shaken by thundering cheers and shouts.

"Long live the god Pharaoh."

Then, Moses threw down his staff, which turned into a huge, frightening snake. The cheers and shouts from the audience for the Pharaoh turned into screams of panic. The blasts of the royal trumpets tried to drown their screams, but the terrifying hiss of the large snake was much louder than they themselves were. The Pharaoh tried to appear steady and confident, as befitted his position as a god, but truly he was shivering with fear where he sat.

The snake reared up high, its mouth wide, and slithered

---

[1] Holy Qur'an, Chapter 26, verse 44.

around the arena. The audience were still screaming in panic, while the Pharaoh was fumbling with one foot, stealthily looking for a sandal that had fallen off at that moment. Suddenly, the snake sank forward on to the ground and swallowed up all those the magicians had made.

At that moment, all the magicians cried out loud and said, "We believe in the Lord of the mankind, Jinns and all that exists, the Lord of Moses and Aaron,"[2] and all of them fell down together, prostrate.

The whole place was in an uproar.

Moses and Aaron left the arena yard as quietly, steadily and peacefully as they had entered it, while the Pharaoh's soldiers moved back to make way for them both, their eyes fixed upon their Pharaoh waiting for any signal to arrest, or even kill, them both.

But the Pharaoh, their so-called god, was busy with himself, wondering how he would get up on his feet again and walk steadily before his people. It seemed that he had lost control over his own senses, so how then could he control his kingdom?

The roaring cascade of cheers and shouts for him had dried up at that moment, just like his saliva had also done; so he grasped a glass with a trembling hand to have a drink of water, while still choking and coughing. Then he stood up, ordered all the magicians to be tortured to death. At the head of his entourage, he left in a hurry to hide his fears.

The chaos spread all over the arena, and people rushed quickly to get out of there. At the same time, the arena yard was jammed with soldiers chaining and arresting all the magicians. The magicians loudly insisted that they now

---

2 Holy Qur'an, Chapter 26, verses 47 and 48

disbelieved in the Pharaoh, and they wouldn't retract this whatsoever. They were 'released' from their bondage to him, and threw away their lives as they had thrown down their ropes and staffs a while earlier.

Samhari hurried among the crowds carrying two of his children, and Malissa, behind him, carried the other one; while Rachel pulled Samatya's arm as she seemed to be absent-minded, as if she didn't want to leave the place unless the flow of the crowds pushed them all out of the arena. With some difficulty, they arrived back at the parking yard and got on the waggon. They moved off slowly till it had passed through the bottleneck caused by the crowd; then, once clear, faster towards home.

On the way they were all silent. Samatya didn't let go of Rachel's hand, and Rachel patted her hand every now and then. It was a silent dialogue between both of them that nobody else could understand, while Malissa leaned her head on Rachel's shoulder and tucked her hand under her arm. Rachel was amidst them like a strong rope to which they all clung fast.

After they had got back to the house, Malissa returned home with her husband and children. Then Samatya and Rachel sat in the garden together, and looked at the sky as the sun was about to set.

That night, the light of the moon and stars changed the darkness of the night into a faded grey colour. Samatya moved the curtains of silence away gently and said in a quiet, soft voice, "I'm missing him so much, mother, as if I haven't seen him in a long time."

"He will be back soon, daughter, after he has finished his work, by God's will," Rachel said.

"Really? And will he know where our place is, mother?"

Samatya asked.

Rachel looked over and asked her back, "Whom are you talking about, daughter?"

"About him, mother: Moses, the prophet of God," Samatya replied.

Rachel smiled and said, "Surely, my dear daughter, he will know where we are. He came to guide us to God's path."

"I want to go to him, mother, to tell him that I believe in him and will follow him with all my heart," Samatya said.

"He conveyed the message, daughter, and you believed it," Rachel said. "Now you have to thank the sender of that message. You should thank Him for it, and always renew your faith in your heart, proclaim it with your tongue that you believed in His prophet and His message. Then, one day we will go together to Moses to thank him for conveying God's message to us honestly, and to tell him how great he was by confronting those tyrants alone steadily; and though we know very well it was God who supported him, we have to thank him too for bearing such a burden for us."

"I'm afraid, mother, those tyrants would kill him," Samatya said.

"If the Pharaoh was able to kill him as he said, daughter, he would kill him. But he did nothing but carry out God's will. So he couldn't kill him and his brother as he did the magicians. Don't you see why—that God comes between the person and his heart's wishes, and prevents him from deciding just anything?"

"But why did he kill the magicians?" Samatya asked.

Rachel replied, "The Pharaoh thought they would be on his side, and would hide what they were quite sure of, which is that Moses *is* a prophet, not a magician; but they let him down. The prostration of those well-versed magicians today was conclusive evidence that Moses is not a magician, and that what everyone saw was not magic, but a miracle from God."

"What do you expect next, mother?" Samatya asked.

Rachel thought quietly for a moment, then replied, "I don't know, daughter. What happened today is not a good sign for what is next, but anyway, God's purpose will surely prevail."

Then Samatya fell into a deep sleep where she sat, as she hadn't slept since the previous day, while Rachel remained awake next to her.

After quite some time, Rachel slept too. All at once, both of them woke up together in panic at hearing the gate slam. It was Hori, who had come back and seemed to be very angry.

Rachel rushed to her room, and Samatya asked him in a quiet voice, "What happened? Are you alright?"

He shouted, "How can I be alright after what happened today? Didn't you see? Didn't you hear the speech? Don't you feel any danger threatens us in our land? After all this, you ask me if I'm alright?"

Samatya realised that he was still wandering blindly in his belief even after what he had seen that day, so she said, "Is this your own point of view?"

"What do you mean?" he asked.

She paused briefly, and tried to rearrange her thoughts. Then she realised that what had happened today before her eyes should not be in vain, and she had to face the falsehood. Also, she remembered the magicians who had sacrificed their souls to defend the truth.

"What do you mean?" he repeated, louder.

She looked at him, and said quietly, "Calm down, Hori. Change your clothes, have your dinner and then we can talk.

All right?"

"Stop trying to avoid answering me!" Hori said angrily.

"I'm not! It's you who's doing the avoiding. Why won't you answer me? Can you tell me what the chief architect's opinion is about what happened today?" Samatya asked.

"It's as same as what the Pharaoh said in his speech," Hori replied.

"That what I wanted you to tell me, and that's why I asked you for your own opinion," Samatya said.

"You knew my opinion very well before I went to work for the chief architect, and it hasn't changed," Hori said.

"Even after what you saw today for yourself?" Samatya asked.

"Ye," Hori replied, turning his eyes away from hers.

"Didn't you think at least briefly about why those magicians sacrificed their own souls while they supposedly supported the Pharaoh? Is it logical that they did that for the sake of a magician?" Samatya asked.

"He is their chief, who taught them magic," Hori replied impatiently.

"Let's suppose you are right," said Samatya, "though it doesn't entirely make sense. If he was truly their chief and taught them magic, as you said, but they then sacrificed their souls for a different, real chief, then your Pharaoh chose them while not knowing who that other chief was, because that was beyond his knowledge. Is he worthy of being thought a god then? A god that didn't know what was going on, and was also taken in?"

He grabbed both her arms tightly, shook her, and shouted angrily, "I've told you many times not to speak badly about him."

"And what if I told you frankly that I *do* disbelieve in your Pharaoh, and that I believe in Moses' God?" Samatya said in a challenging tone.

He pushed her backwards, and slapped her so violently that she fell down on the ground. Hori was astounded at what he had done. It was the first time he had ever done any such thing. He rushed into his room, and slammed the door so hard that all the house shook.

Samatya stayed where she was, her eyes flooded with tears that drowned her cheeks. She raised them towards the sky. Rachel was crying inside her room. The silence of the night had allowed her to hear everything.

Samatya felt a severe chill. It was now late. She gathered her wits, stood up, and walked sluggishly towards Rachel's room. No sooner had she entered than she threw herself into Rachel's arms and wept. Rachel wept with her.

CHAPTER XVI

The Three Friends

The next morning, Samatya woke up, heard Hori going out to work and shutting the house gate; but neither of them saw the other. Perhaps last night was just a page that could be closed, and that with a new day, a new page could be opened; or perhaps that last night was itself the start of something. Nobody could say.

What had happened in the Celebration Arena was still alive in all people's eyes, dwelt in their minds, and occupied their daily conversations. They broke up into sects: pros, who were reticent; disbelievers, who were mocking; and those who declared their faith were exposed to anger and plots visited upon them by disbelievers. The gaps increased, day by day, among neighbours, friends, and even members of the same family for the same reason, and for nothing else.

Malissa went to work as usual in the Pharaoh's palace. All workers were busy, each at her own task, but their conversation never stopped. The topic of their conversation was the same, like yesterday and the day before that. One of them was saying bad things about the prophet Moses, while the rest were laughing and mocking him too, which only encouraged her to continue. But in so doing, she exceeded all limits concerning the prophet to such an extent that she crossed a line which should not have been crossed, by any *creature* whatsoever.

After hearing her workfellow, Malissa could no longer endure the burden of her silence. It was as if she was wearing a heavy winter dress in August while standing in front of the stove in that kitchen. All at once, she took it off, threw it in their faces, and burst out shouting at them all.

All her workfellows in the kitchen gathered together against her. Eventually, Malissa's hidden faith was discovered, and became clear to everyone. She simply defended her belief and the prophet, and reminded them of the miracle that all of them had seen, but she didn't get any response but mocking. She was keen to bring other proof for them, rather than the miracle itself, in order to convince them and make them believe; but all she found were her tears, while they stood in front of her like idols. She rushed out of the kitchen, weeping, and left the place—and headed to Samatya's house.

Samatya and Rachel got panicky because of her unexpected visit, especially when they saw the state she was in, and they wondered what had happened. Malissa told them the whole story.

The situation back in the kitchen, though, was much more complicated than Malissa could have imagined. They had complained about her to their chief supervisor, who in turn reported to the Pharaoh's daughter, who rushed and informed the Pharaoh himself. A royal decree was issued at once to set fire to Malissa's house and to kill all her family, too, as a lesson to all others.

Soldiers descended upon Malissa's village like a storm and asked where her house was. The people there wondered what had happened. One of her neighbours said, "She is a good woman and wouldn't hurt anyone." No sooner had she finished speaking than one of the soldiers whipped her for defending Malissa. Then they set fire to the entire house. The smoke rose high into the sky, and one of the soldiers shouted, "This is her reward for disbelieving in the great god Pharaoh."

Her neighbours got frightened, volunteering, even competing with each other to tell the soldiers that she wasn't inside the house as she hadn't yet come back from work, and no one was there inside the house but her children.

At that moment, Samhari was on his way back home. He started to run in panic towards his house as he spotted the smoke drifting up into the sky.

The neighbours were still behaving treacherously in front of the soldiers, so that as soon as they saw Samhari getting closer, they pointed him out to the soldiers. The soldiers killed him at once, and moved off quickly looking for Malissa although nobody knew where she was.

The soldiers returned to the palace, and informed their commander that their mission had been partly successful, but Malissa was not to be found. The news spread all over the palace, while Hori was there with the chief architect who was in a meeting with the Pharaoh. He didn't show any reaction, as if he neither knew Malissa nor her children whom he had played with only a few days earlier.

Then, after he finished work, he returned home. He heard Malissa's voice coming from Rachel's room. He called to Samatya, and she came out of Rachel's room quietly. He beckoned to her to follow him to their room.

"I don't know how to start," he said in a low voice.

"It's not the right time now," Samatya replied. "Let's talk later after Malissa leaves."

"I didn't mean what you're thinking. I want to talk about

something else; a very serious matter that can't be put off," Hori said.

Samatya wondered, and said, "What is it?"

He told her what had happened. She started to scream, but he bent down over her and pressed his hand to her mouth to stifle her screams. Then he whispered to her.

"Don't scream. Now's not the time. The matter is too serious. They are looking for her now to kill her. If they know that she's here, they will kill all of us. Do you understand? She has to leave right now. I can't do anything for her but to let her go to a safe place. Don't ever tell her what happened to her children and husband, do you hear me? I will remove my hand now, but don't scream. Do you hear me?"

Samatya nodded to him that she agreed, while her tears ran over and drowned his hand. No sooner had he taken his hand from her mouth than she fell down on her knees, silently weeping and sobbing. Hori knelt down in front of her and said in a quiet, sad tone, "Time is passing so quickly. She has to leave soon. I know very well that this is hard for you, but I have no other choice, Samatya. I will go back to work now. When I return home, I want to hear from you that she has already left. Please, Samatya, I don't want anyone to be hurt, so don't do anything other than what I just told you."

Samatya tried hard to speak, but her voice was choked by tears. "Rest assured I will do what you said."

He patted her hand and said, "You must know that, whatever happens between you and me, my love for you will never, ever change. I can't remove it from my heart, either willingly or unwillingly. Also, I can't force my heart to accept anything unwillingly. I hope you understand what I mean, Samatya."

He cupped her cheeks with both hands, kissed her forehead

and departed, leaving the weight of the world on her shoulders. She stayed rooted to the spot, not knowing what to do other than weep.

Then she remembered that she has been through difficulties before, when no one could help her except One who was truly able to help. She prayed before an unknown god that she was still looking for, but at that moment she prayed with all her heart to her Lord whom she believed in, and believed in His prophet too. She prayed to her Lord with just two words in which there was a mighty strength that would be able to bear the whole earth and all that was on or in it—even the mountains themselves—so easily; and she said, "O Lord!"

Then she called Rachel with a quivering breath. They rushed in together, Rachel with Malissa, in panic. When Samatya saw Malissa, she hugged her and sobbed, while the two friends didn't know what had happened.

"What is the matter, Samatya?" Malissa asked.

Rachel tried to find out what had happened too, but to no avail. Samatya gathered her thoughts, as she knew that she had no choice but to be strong, and said, "We must leave this place now, all of us. We have no time."

Rachel and Malissa looked at each other, not understanding.

"Hori told me that your workfellows in the kitchen tattled on you to the Pharaoh, and they are looking for you now to kill you. No time for details. We must go now," Samatya said angrily through her tears.

Malissa was in a state of shock and saying nothing, while Rachel said, "Hurry up, Malissa. You and I must go now to my village, and you stay here, Samatya, with your husband. There's no need for you to come with us, daughter."

Samatya refused to stay and insisted on going with them.

Malissa said in a quiet voice, "You stay here, Samatya. I will go alone with mother."

Samatya became angry again, and said, "How can I let you go alone? Did I prevent you from being with me in my most difficult time, or I did come to you myself and have you support me? I swear by God, I won't leave you to go alone, Malissa. But there's no time to talk about it. Let's go now, please."

Then Rachel suggested to them both that they disguise themselves in some of her clothes to look as if they were all from the Children of Israel. They hurried up, changed their clothes, left quickly all together, and headed to the village of the Children of Israel.

In the evening, Hori returned home late. He was thinking about what Samatya would have done. When he got inside the house, it was deadly silent. He was shocked to see the cabinet open, and none of Samatya's clothes in there. He couldn't believe his eyes—and rushed to Rachel's room, where there was nothing either.

He hurried out to the garden to his waggon, but suddenly he stopped. He could not take even one step forward, as it was impossible for him to gamble with Samatya's life, so he retreated. He was somewhat reassured when he remembered what Samatya had told him before: that she'd gone with Malissa to Rachel's house in her village to bring her, so he knew that they would have all gone there together now, as it was the only place that would be safe for them all.

He sat in to the garden, and noticed the green colour starting to cover all the soil. He smiled sadly, and touched those plants gently—Samatya's plants—and his eyes shone with tears. Then he turned and looked back towards the house. It wasn't as beautiful as it had been before, as if it was frowning at him. Everything had changed.

Hori remained awake where he was till early next morning; he couldn't go inside to their room because Samatya was not there. Then he could not resist his drowsiness any more, and he fell asleep in the garden.

CHAPTER XVII

A Rising Star

The next day, Malissa's workfellows' conversation dripped malice as they gloated over what had happened to her family, but they were still full of malice against her for having escaped death, and because no one could find her. Each one showed the depths of her sick imagination: one said she might have thrown herself in the river after she'd found out what had happened to her family; another said she might have been burnt inside her house with her children …

Then another one said confidently that she was the one who had the true news. She knew from Malissa's neighbour, who had told her that Malissa had a friend there in the city, called Samatya; and her husband worked as a personal bodyguard to the chief architect.

They unanimously agreed that Malissa must be hiding in Samatya's house. Then they informed their chief supervisor about their conclusion.

No sooner had the news got out than soldiers were hurriedly sent to Hori's house. Hori woke up in panic hearing the soldiers knocking on the gate, He opened up, and said in a wondering tone, "What is wrong?"

"Good morning, Hori," the commander said. "I'm sorry I have to carry out these commands, but you know the rules well enough," and he beckoned to the soldiers to inspect the house. The soldiers immediately rushed inside, while the commander explained the matter to Hori.

After a while the soldiers came out and told their commander that nobody was inside.

"Then you have to come with me, Hori, for investigation," the commander said.

Hori went with them, quietly and without any objection, to the city security headquarters. After quite some time waiting, he and the commander went into the room of the chief general of city security, Nakht.

He was an old man, and was known for his sharp wit and intelligence that everybody feared, not because he was big-bodied, nor because he was harsh-faced. On the contrary, he was a short and skinny man, with a cunning smile that always covered his quiet face, and his eyes shone with cleverness. Beside him sat one of his assistants, Akhnu.

Then Hori entered with the commander. Nakht beckoned to the commander to dismiss him, while he examined Hori with sharp looks.

"Where is your wife, Hori?" Nakht asked quietly.

"I don't know, sir," Hori replied.

With an ironic smile, Nakht looked at his assistant Akhnu while he was addressing Hori, and said, "Do you really think you can convince me that you don't know where your wife is?"

"Believe me, sir, I don't know," Hori replied. "I left her at home and went to work yesterday. When I returned home, I couldn't find her."

"Once upon a time, a man came back home from his work and couldn't find his wife, then he didn't even bother to look for her till the next day," Nakht said sarcastically; then anger appeared in his voice, and he said, "Are you joking, young man?"

Hori realised that he was not in front of an easy man at all. There was no place for evasion, so he decided to tell him almost all the truth; but there was one thing he would keep to himself, something that nobody would find out even if he were killed.

"I will tell you the whole truth, sir," he said. "I don't deny that Malissa is a close friend of my wife. She used to visit us, and my wife used to visit her too. Yesterday, at work, I heard what happened to Malissa because she disbelieved in our great god Pharaoh. I was afraid to tell anybody that I knew her, as I would be accused of being a disbeliever too, which I have never ever dared to even think about. Then, I returned home, and didn't find my wife there, and then I found out that she had taken all her clothes and left the house. She didn't even tell me that she would be going out. Eventually, I was quite sure that my wife had gone to see Malissa, and died there at her house too."

Nakht was convinced somewhat by what Hori said, but he didn't let him see that. "Rest assured, Hori," he said. "Your wife is still alive, and her friend too. They are both fugitives. They must both be killed. The same fate awaits whoever hides them."

"I know that very well, sir," Hori said. "I've told you all that I know, and it is for you to command, sir."

Nakht looked him in the eye for a while, and said, "You can go now, Hori."

Hori went out and headed directly to his work as he was late. He told the chief architect about everything that had happened to him. The chief architect told Hori that he knew all the details, and reassured him that he would protect him as he trusted him. That was how it seemed to Hori, anyway; but, unknown to him, all his movements were under scrutiny in the belief that he might lead them to Samatya and Malissa.

The days passed slowly. Hori tried to bury himself in his work, but deep inside him grief settled in and occupied his soul day and night. He felt that he was under supervision, although he didn't show it, but he acted as normally as possible. He knew well that they wanted to reach Samatya, and then Malissa, through him, but Samatya's life was more precious to him than anything else, which was how he tolerated the bitterness of being away from her.

Nearly one year elapsed. Hori was doing a commendable job. Surveillance also was lifted, as it seemed to them he didn't know where his wife was. Although Hori felt that he was no longer under supervision, he didn't change his normal routine as they might be plotting against him, so he had to plot against them too.

One day, the chief architect surprised Hori by promoting him to the position of chief commander of guards over all his palaces. Hori pretended to be happy about the promotion, but at heart he hadn't tasted happiness since Samatya left.

Days passed, and Hori's rising star began to shine clearly on the horizon, news of which reached the Pharaoh himself courtesy of the chief architect, who had told the Pharaoh the whole story of Hori, that he was a smart man and trustworthy. Also, he told him that Hori was a faithful believer, and he did not even care about his wife when he knew that she was a disbeliever and had run away with her friend Malissa. At that time, the Pharaoh himself had already tortured his own wife to death as she believed in the Lord of Moses, so he was very pleased with Hori, to the extent that he at once issued a royal decree assigning Hori the position of deputy to the chief general of city security, Nakht. Besides, Nakht was getting old, and performance reports about his assistants, including Akhnu, did not indicate that any of them would be fit to be his successor.

"What an excellent selection, my holy lord," the chief architect said to the Pharaoh.

That day, Hori returned home still unable to believe his ears. It was more than he could ever imagine, especially within that short period of time.

Eventually, happiness knocked on his door, but no sooner had he intended to open up and let it in than he noticed Samatya's plant in the garden, that now stood straight on its stem. At once, he knelt down next to it and cried. He was missing her so much; he was craving, dying, to see her. He thought, for a while, about rushing over to Rachel's village; but he swiftly backed away from that idea, and killed it in its cradle. He was still afraid of losing her forever, and said to himself, "It is not time yet."

One day, Hori was at his work's headquarters in a meeting with Nakht and Akhnu. They were discussing a new plan to secure the city internally more efficiently, within a major plan to tighten up control over the whole country in anticipation of any external attack, and all according to the Pharaoh's instructions.

All at once, Nakht fell unconscious in his chair. It was clear that he was over-exhausted. Hori rushed and summoned his private physician, who came immediately and checked him till he had recovered slightly.

"He must be transferred now to his mansion," the physician said.

Hori ordered Akhnu to stay, and told him that he himself would accompany Nakht to his mansion with the physician. He carried Nakht himself from the meeting room out to his private waggon. After they arrived at Nakht's mansion, Hori also carried him from the waggon to his room as well.

Aya, the daughter of Nakht, cried to see her father like that. While he was laying Nakht on his bed, Hori reassured her that he was alright, and she had to be strong for him if she wanted him to recover soon. Nakht was looking helplessly at his daughter and the physician next to him.

After some time Nakht fell asleep, and the physician said to Aya, "He is better right now, but he has to stay in bed for some days and to take his medicine on time. I will pass by every now and then to check on him." Then he excused himself and left. A while after, Hori asked Aya to allow him to visit Nakht later. She smiled to let him know that she welcomed his request. Then he excused himself too, and left.

Aya was the only daughter of Nakht. She was nearly twenty, had lost her mother years ago, and lived alone with her father. She was particularly attractive, an icon of African beauty; it was very clear in her distinctive smile, looks, and her tone of voice as well.

Aya stayed beside her father till he woke up, then she asked the chaperones to bring both his food and her food too, so as to have lunch with him.

"You are exhausting yourself at work, father," she said. "You have to take some rest, please. It is time to quit. I have been missing you a lot since my childhood. Your work has taken up most of your time."

He patted her hand and said in a weak voice, "I can't, Aya. If I quit I would die, daughter."

Then she tried to direct their conversation little by little towards Hori, as she wanted to know more about him. Her father realised that, and told her everything about Hori while she listened with great interest. Then she left him to let him have some rest, and went to her room. All her thoughts were centred on Hori, and each day she expected him to come as he said; and she gave greater importance to making herself look more elegant.

Eventually, Hori came for a visit. She received him herself, accompanied him to her father's room, and stayed with them the whole time. The way she looked at Hori gave away her admiration of him, but Hori avoided her gaze most of the time. After a short time, he made his excuses to leave, and she accompanied him to the door and showed him out. When she returned to her father, she kept talking all the time about him. But it was the last visit for Hori as her father completely recovered and returned to work.

Later on, Nakht spotted the sadness in Aya's eyes. It was clear to him that she had cried a lot and not slept well either. He asked her chaperone about her. She told him that Aya would hardly eat, and no one knew why.

Day after day, Aya was getting worse. Nakht asked her why. She didn't reply, but cried. Then, he thought of something, so he tried to talk to her about Hori. She got confused, and turned her eyes away from his. At that moment, he was quite sure that his daughter was deeply in love with Hori. He realised that Aya had grown up enough to get married, and said to himself, "Why doesn't she get married to Hori?"

Since he had been promoted to his new position, Hori had a private mansion, but he kept the old house too. Every now and then he had to go there in order to take care of Samatya's plants. For him it was like a holy visit to a temple in which he practised the rituals of his love for Samatya.

He did not know what was being planned for him. Nakht still had the same idea in mind. He took his time and decided.

One day, after a meeting, Hori excused himself to leave to his room, but Nakht asked him to stay. "I want to talk with you, Hori, about something important," Nakht said, and beckoned to him to sit down.

Hori got worried and sat down quietly.

"Why haven't you got married again by now? Your wife ran away, and you know what she and her friend did."

Hori got very worried by such an unexpected question after all that time. He thought that Nakht knew where Samatya was, and knew that he had lied to him as well. He tried hard to hide his worries and fears, and began to reply, but Nakht interrupted him.

"You may consider my question an interference into your personal life, but I consider myself as your father, Hori."

Hori calmed down a little bit, but he was still worried, and said, "Sir, it does indeed please me that you are interested in my personal life, but I really don't have time to think about that matter now. And who would accept marriage to a man like me who spends all his time on his work?"

"And what if she exists, and agrees?" Nakht asked.

Hori smiled. He thought that Nakht was joking with him.

"You are a smart and successful man, Hori. You remind me of myself when I was your age," Nakht said. Then, he suddenly asked him, "Would you agree to marry my daughter, Hori?"

Hori's face was suffused with happiness—not because he would marry Aya, but because his worries were completely melted away. "It's a great honour, sir, that I wouldn't even have dared to dream of," Hori said.

Nakht was very pleased with Hori's reply and said, "Well, prepare yourself for your wedding party soon."

Later the same day, Hori left his work headquarters, surrounded by his soldiers till he had got on his waggon, beckoning to the driver to move off. As soon as he arrived at his mansion, the guard hurried and opened the gate. Hori climbed down from the waggon, and headed to the inner stairs to his room. On his way, the chief housekeeper told him that lunch was ready, but he beckoned to her that he didn't want to eat.

No sooner had he entered his room and shut the door than he cried hard. He felt that he was enchained, deprived of his beloved wife, that he couldn't even dare to go anywhere near. He thought once again about going to her, but he remembered that they would then both be killed.

The days passed quickly. Hori and Aya got married in a big ceremony, and they lived with Nakht in his mansion at his request. Aya was so very happy, doing anything and everything that would make Hori happy. However, Hori was only apparently happy, like a gorgeous palace from the outside, but which inside was abandoned and ruined.

As usual, at a specific time, fate imposed its will, making no distinction between rich or poor. Aya's happiness did not last forever. She lost her father, as if she had fallen from flying high; and broke down and wept.

At the same time, Hori took over Nakht's position, and became the chief general of city security, and became one of those who were very close to the Pharaoh himself. And before Hori could open up all the doors of his heart to happiness, happiness invaded his heart itself: eventually he was able to see Samatya, and who could prevent him?

CHAPTER XVIII

The Old Man

It was there, where the forgotten people were; the ones who had slipped out of other people's memory, and were neglected by them; the ones who the Pharaoh himself was wary of.

There, in village of the Children of Israel.

It was a wintry night full of rain. All the roads were muddy, and all the people there shrank back inside their homes. Darkness covered the village, the sun having set only a short time earlier; but dark clouds covered the sky, and the moon was hidden behind them.

Samatya was hiding there as well, but behind a black cloak to keep out the severe cold, that nearly covered all of her. She sat on the ground, drew her legs towards her chest and leaned with her head on her crossed arms.

Next to her, Malissa lay on her back on the ground. She was not as she had been before. She looked quite different, having become skinny, pale and sunken-eyed. No one would ever have recognised her unless they had known her very well before. Her wide-open eyes stared at nothing, or so it seemed to Samatya, Rachel, or any other human being who saw her.

Since she had learned what had happened to her children and husband, she neither screamed nor cried, but she had been hit hard by the news. Unless Rachel and Samatya urged her to have some food and water, she never asked for either.

Sometimes she did respond, as if she didn't know what they were doing to her, but most of the time not at all.

Rachel sat on the other side of Malissa, re-covering her each time the cover slipped down off her, while Malissa neither felt the severe cold nor the cover itself.

Samatya was still thinking of Hori. It pained her to remember what he'd done the last time she'd seen him, but later on she realised that he had been quite right; that he had saved all their lives. She had eventually reached that conclusion after Rachel convinced her. Rachel was the only one who knew, from Benjamin, everything that had happened regarding Hori, but she hid all that from Samatya, especially the news of his marriage.

Samatya reminded herself all the time that Rachel had lost her twins and husband defending her faith, and that Malissa had lost *her* children and husband for doing the same thing. If she lost Hori, the same thing would not happen to her. But the main reason for her grief was that she was still in love with him; and she was afraid that he would remain a disbeliever, so that she would lose him both in this life and the life hereafter as well. Also, she became aware that wisdom was not to *know* the right way, but to walk in it in trust. Thus she surrendered to God's command.

Thus, the three friends' lives were spent in Rachel's house. Nearly all days were the same; they didn't go out of the house other than for necessities. The money and gold that Samatya had brought with her were about to run out, especially as none of them had done any work since they had come to Rachel's house. Benjamin and his wife were the only people they knew and trusted; they kept their secret, and were taking care of them as well.

That evening, Hori decided to go to Samatya, after a long time thinking about how he would go and return, safely. He went to his old house and, disguised as an old man from the Children of Israel, he rented a waggon and headed to Rachel's village.

When Hori arrived there, he asked the waggoner to wait for him. He knocked on a door to ask where Rachel's house was, very worried that she might not have been there in the village. But the door was opened at once, and the owner of that house told him where hers was. The sound of his heart beating was louder than thunder itself, such was his fear that he would not find Samatya with her.

He reached Rachel's house, and knocked on her door with a trembling hand. This frightened both Rachel and Samatya.

"It must be Benjamin," Rachel said.

"What brought him at such a time?" Samatya said.

"You stay here. I will check, daughter," Rachel said.

No sooner had Rachel partially opened the door, cautiously, than he pushed the door quickly, entered, and shut it again, removed the beard and moustache of his face and said, "It is me, Hori, Mother. Where is Samatya?"

Samatya, inside the room, didn't believe her ears. She rushed out quickly. As soon as Hori saw her he rushed towards her too. She threw herself into his arms, and they hugged each other and cried hard for all the years that had separated them from each other.

Rachel left them, and went inside with Malissa, held her hand which was as cold as ice, kissed it, embraced it with both her hands to give it some warmth, and cried, which Malissa did not understand.

Little by little the euphoria of their reunion subsided, and

Samatya began to blame Hori for everything, although she knew deep in her heart that he was right. But it seemed that she had a plan.

"Did you want me to keep Malissa at our house? Did you know that the next morning they took me for investigation, and they were looking for you to kill you as well?" Hori said.

"You didn't even think about seeing me all that time, did you?" Samatya said.

"Sweetie, it wasn't because I didn't care about you. On the contrary, it was I cared almost *too* much about you and your life. I was under probation, Samatya, all the time."

"And how did you manage to come now, while you are under probation?" Samatya asked.

"I came to you in disguise—as you can see—to be quite sure that no one would know me," Hori replied.

"Why didn't you come in disguise before, then?" Samatya asked.

"I told you; I was under probation, but now I'm safe, and disguised for more security as well," Hori replied

At this point, Samatya didn't know that she was interrogating the chief general of the city security himself, but Hori was happy to be interrogated by his beloved wife. Then, he told her everything but one thing: he hid from her his marriage to Aya.

Samatya couldn't believe what she was hearing. It was like a fairy tale to her. She said, "For the first time in my life, I feel I'm scared of you, Hori."

Hori didn't like the sound of that. He hugged her, and said, "Samatya, how can you say that? You will never know how much you mean to me."

"Your loyalty to the Pharaoh may one day make you come

and kill us all," Samatya said.

Hori rose up angrily and said, "If that were the case, I would have killed you a long time ago, Samatya."

"Then your love for me is greater than your loyalty to the Pharaoh?" Samatya asked.

He didn't answer her. There were more questions, the only answer to which was silence.

"Has the time not come yet, Hori? Please, darling, just think; not for me, but for the sake of the truth. Take your time and think. I know well you feel torn by what I say. I promise you I will never say it again."

He didn't comment on what she had said, but he asked her about Malissa. She told him that she felt nothing towards anyone or anything, and it was God's mercy upon her.

Then, he asked her to stay in Rachel's house to be safe, and promised that he would pass by every now and then to see her. He gave her a lot of money and prepared to leave. He put back the beard and the moustache on to his face, kissed her hands and hugged her, while she smiled at seeing him like that; then cried.

He opened the door very cautiously and left quickly. Flashes of lightning lit up the whole village, as if to guide him on his way back.

CHAPTER XIX

Asmaya

Hori's successive secret visits to the Children of Israel's village continued. Each time he returned home, he felt ever more secure because he was reassured about Samatya. So his visits to Samatya were a fuel that made him able to carry on.

He was keen to achieve not only the security of the whole city, but also the security of Samatya.

The years began to fly. All the country suffered from successive disasters, which the people thought were because of the magic of Moses. Each time they promised him that they would believe, after he had stopped a disaster, but each time they failed in their promise.

One evening, Hori sat next to Aya, each one of them thinking of different things. He was thinking of those successive disasters that had happened over the last years, and said to himself, "If Moses was truly a magician, and it was him who caused those disasters, and it was him who lifted them as well, then he would possess a supernatural power. Why didn't he use such power to eliminate the Pharaoh himself? And why did he give the Pharaoh all those years?"

Then, he remembered what Samatya had said to him: *"Please, darling, just think; not for me, but for the sake of the truth. Take your time, and think."*

He thought of Samatya herself and her attitude towards

her friend Malissa: that she had sacrificed him, her love, her life, and run away with her. He also thought about Malissa, how much she loved Samhari and her children, but had lost them all.

He thought of someone who was better placed than Samatya and Malissa: the wife of the Pharaoh himself. With her velvet life, she didn't have to care about threats by the Pharaoh himself, of being tortured to death; and for whom? For Moses the magician?

He remembered the magicians who had declared their faith and were tortured to death too. Again he wondered for whom? Moses did not give any reward to any of them. Did the wife of the Pharaoh expect a reward from a magician? Did Samatya have a reward from Moses while she lived all those years in such a humble house as Rachel's?

Then, he fell into a deep sleep. Aya was next to him, thinking about the delay in her becoming pregnant. She had been consulting with the midwives and seeking the blessings of gods and goddesses at temples over the last years, but uselessly. Hori was eager to have a child too. His dream of having a child had never stopped. He would have liked to have a child with either Aya or Samatya, but at heart he wished to have him with Samatya. It seemed to have been decreed that neither Aya nor Samatya would get pregnant yet for a reason.

One day, Hori returned from work to find Aya impatiently waiting to surprise him with the good news that he was going be a father.

"I will name him Hori if it's a boy, and Asmaya if it's a girl," Aya said.

Hori smiled and said, "And what about me, Aya? Why

can't I name even just one of them?"

"Because you won't get tired bringing them up as you won't be there all the time. It is the mother who gets very tired bringing children up, darling," Aya replied.

Hori laughed and said, "You're absolutely right, and I do agree with you, Aya."

The days passed so fast. Hori was at work in a meeting with his two assistants, Akhnu and Horemheb.

Akhnu was an assistant to Nakht, and had dreamt of taking over Nakht's position one day. Also, he loved Aya, and had planned to get closer to her, but he was too late. Later on, he couldn't make any objection when Hori took over the position of Nakht instead of him, as it was the Pharaoh's royal decree; but he kept it to himself, waiting for an opportunity to come. His grudge towards Hori increased after his marriage to Aya, since Hori had taken everything he dreamt of, but he couldn't do anything yet.

Horemheb was a quiet, wise leader, who was selected by Hori himself to be one of his assistants; and, unlike Akhnu, he was loyal to Hori. But what Hori didn't know about Horemheb was that he knew Samatya very well. He was one of the villagers who loved her in silence and never told anyone, especially after she had got married to Hori. He didn't get married because of his love for Samatya. He still hid his love for her in the same way as he hid his faith. And Samatya didn't even know him.

During that meeting, one of the guards at Hori's mansion hurried over to see him. Hori didn't feel reassured when he spotted him. The guard told him that his lady was in labour and had asked to see him. Hori rushed with him to the mansion at once. Horemheb and Akhnu looked at each other; it was the first time they had thought the same thing together at the same time.

No sooner had Hori arrived there than he felt a chill run him. He saw that the chaperones were crying; and, eventually, the midwife came to him, looking down at the floor, and said in a sad voice, "I'm sorry to tell you, sir, that lady Aya has just passed away, but she has given birth to a beautiful healthy girl."

Hori hugged his daughter, and wept heavily. Through his tears, he said that Aya had never done anything other than to always make him happy; and he was sad for his daughter as she would never see or know her mother. He gently gave the chief chaperone his daughter, naming her as he did so, and said, "I don't want any one of you to neglect Asmaya even for a moment. Do you hear me?"

Still crying herself, she nodded *yes*, and took Asmaya from him.

That same evening, Hori went to visit Samatya and found her in tears. He wondered why; then she told him that Malissa had passed away a few days earlier. Hori's own tears began to fall, to the extent that Samatya wondered why he was crying like that. It was not because of Malissa's death. She couldn't figure it out at that moment, but she was quite sure that he was hiding something.

CHAPTER XX

The Unexpected

The days passed lazily, and Hori grew ever more concerned for Asmaya, because of his having to spend most of the time at his work and leave her alone with the chaperones. Deep down in his heart, he wished to send Asmaya to live with Samatya, and that he would never find a substitute mother for her other than Samatya. But, he did not dare to tell her that. Also, he felt the strain of having to keep his visits to Samatya secret, as he wished her to be close to him forever as well.

Samatya's voice was echoing inside his head. *Then your love for me is greater than your loyalty to the Pharaoh?*

Then he said to himself, "Yes, my love for you is greater than my loyalty to the Pharaoh himself." Then he began to rebuke himself. "Shame on you! How good a leader can you be if you feel so scared that you don't even dare to confront a woman? You don't dare explain to Samatya that you'd got married again, and why. Is this love or cowardice? How much of a coward are you?"

He turned away from his bewilderment, and headed over to see Samatya. He decided to tell her everything. No sooner did she see him than she looked into his eyes, and tried to read what was written there. She did not find anything; no words, just his confusion, from which she could read nothing. She didn't even ask him what was on his mind, but gave him time, as she was quite sure that those words had made him tongue-tied, and he was struggling to speak.

He asked her about herself, as the sadness was quite clearly etched upon her face since Malissa had passed away.

"Thank God for everything," Samatya replied quietly; but as soon as she uttered it, she expected him to get angry with her. But he smiled, patted her hand and said, "Do you remember our evenings by the river, in our first old house, Samatya?"

She kept quiet for a while, and then burst into tears, as if he touched an unhealed wound. She remembered Malissa and her support that first, hard night.

Hori embraced her. Then she remembered his question and said, "I wish that you had never travelled to the south, Hori."

Hori wept so uncontrollably that she decided to ask him what was wrong; but at that moment he began to speak himself, and said, "There is something you should know, Samatya."

He told her everything. She closed her eyes, choked back her tears and kept silent for quite some time; then she moved away from him.

"I know it is hard and painful for you, but I know very well that I have never ever loved anyone but you, Samatya. All I ask you for now is for Asmaya to be with you. I am at work all the time, and I don't want to leave her among chaperones. You are the only one that Asmaya should be with."

"You want me to be a chaperone for your daughter, then?" Samatya asked.

"Don't ever say that, Samatya. But I need you to be her mother," Hori replied.

"But I'm not her mother. Her mother is the one who you got married to. At that time you forced me out of your life, and didn't even know where I was. You were quite sure that I would never leave Malissa alone. I expected you to leave everything and to protect *us* at that particular time, as she'd lost her husband. But you chose your own way, and went back to your work, and they were much too generous to you. They granted you everything: a position, a mansion, and a wife too. And what about me? As you see, I have been here, neglected, for years.

"Eventually, after you had enjoyed your life, suddenly you came back to look for me, pretending that you missed me. I was just a thing like all the other things that were once in your life, just like those evenings in the old house. *Then* you ask me to be a chaperone for your daughter. What do you expect me to say?"

"It's all contrary to what you think, Samatya," Hori said. "All the time you were away from me, I have never tasted any happiness. I insisted that Malissa should have to leave, because I knew what would happen to all of us.

"And, if I was looking for such a position and life, and if I was satisfied with it, I would not have come here disguised, and having to look behind me like a thief. I saved all our lives, Samatya, and that was the price."

"Don't try to justify what you have done. I expected you to come and kill us all out of your loyalty to your Pharaoh, but I never expected that you would get married as well, while I was suffering here.

"Do you remember what you said to me on the last day before I went? You told me that your heart was not in your hands, and that you couldn't accept anything unwillingly; and

I tell you now, Hori, that my heart has changed too, so that I can't forgive you unwillingly."

Samatya's words were like a dagger in Hori's heart. He kept quiet while she continued.

"Thank God how lucky I am that He forced His enemies to protect me against their will, but still willingly," she said. "It was not your so-called love for me that prevented you from telling tales on us to your Pharaoh, but it was God's will, only, that forced you to protect us without realising that you were doing so yourself. It was only God's will that set a seal on your Pharaoh's and his soldiers' eyes and hearts, as He did before to your Pharaoh, and made him bring up His prophet Moses in his palace. What a god you worship! It seems that you were not given a portion of your name, Hori. What an irony that your name is Hori while you are a slave to a misguided Pharaoh. It was you, and others like you, who made such a Pharaoh. Woe to you all."

Then she stood up angrily, and went inside.

Hori stayed where he was, Her words were like a burden, thrown on his shoulders, that was so heavy he was unable to stand up. As if she hadn't forgotten his slapping her before, she had slapped him back, in a different way but more violently.

Rachel sat beside the window, not knowing what had happened outside. "Did Hori leave, daughter?" she asked.

"Who is Hori? I don't know anyone by that name," Samatya replied.

Rachel got worried hearing that, and said, "What did you say, Samatya?"

"What you heard, mother," Samatya replied quietly.

Rachel rushed outside to Hori, and said, "What happened, son?"

Hori told her everything that had happened between him and Samatya. She thought quietly for a moment, and said in a low voice that Samatya could not hear, "I knew about all your news, son, from Benjamin, but I kept it all from Samatya. It was easier for me to see her worried about you than to shock her with news of your marriage. She has the right to get angry, and to take her time as well. But for myself, son, I do believe you, and God won't waste what you have done for all of us." Then she patted his hand and added, "Rest assured, son, and leave her to me. I will try with her later. Now you go and bring Asmaya to me, if you want to. I will take care of her myself, even if Samatya herself doesn't agree."

Hori held Rachel's hands, kissed them, and said, "How great you are, mother."

"Don't ever say that, son," she replied. "We don't do anything but God's will. Go and bring her any time you like."

Hori left while he was trying to balance Samatya's wounding and Rachel's favour.

Rachel went to Samatya in her room, where she sat silent and frozen-faced. "I want to talk to you, daughter," Rachel said.

Samatya looked at her silently, as if asking her to go ahead.

"Hori told me everything. But before I start talking, do you want me to please you, or to please God?" Rachel asked.

"You know the answer to that very well, mother," Samatya replied.

"Well, you know that Hori protected us all. You yourself admitted it before, but the reason for your anger now is just because of his marriage.

"I'm quite sure that he loves you very much, because if he was satisfied with his new marriage, he would never gamble his life and come here to see you so many times while his wife was alive. He gambled everything just to see you again, Samatya. And I know well that you still love him too," Rachel said.

Samatya interrupted her and said, "Mother, you know very well how much I appreciate you. But please, I don't want to talk about this matter any more."

"I will pray for you, daughter. But you have to know something: I asked Hori to bring his daughter for me to take care of myself."

Samatya was shocked at what Rachel said. She again went quiet for a moment, and then said, "It is not my right, mother, even to comment on something that belongs to you only."

CHAPTER XXI

The Exodus from Egypt

Hori returned home with Samatya's verbal wound in his ears. He had expected her undoubtedly to be angry with his marriage news, but he had never expected what she then said. He felt for the first time that he had lost a powerful support in his life. But there was nothing he could do. He said to himself, "Our hearts are not in our hands. What about the hearts of others, then."

He changed his mind, and decided to leave Asmaya with her chaperones, but he still felt grateful for Rachel's offer. How great she was that she had offered to do something for him that the one closest to him had refused to. He wished deep in his heart to reward Rachel, but nothing could requite her for such a favour.

It was a most difficult night for Hori; he was in severe need of support. When he remembered Samatya, he turned his face as if looking away, angrily, for the first time. He felt that he missed Aya so much. He went to Asmaya's room, kept watching her innocent face, wondered about her unknown future, kissed her and returned again to his room. He remained awake for a long time thinking deeply; he reached no conclusion, and fell into sleep.

On the following morning, he went to work as usual, where he was told that there was a message from the Pharaoh's palace for him, which stated that he had to go there urgently at noon that day. He went there on time, to find that the Pharaoh had summoned all the state senior officials for a big meeting.

The Pharaoh was exceedingly angry. He told them all that they had to find a solution to prevent any more of those disasters which the whole country had been suffering from over the last few years, otherwise it would surely lead to the downfall of the whole state. They were also not to stand around idly waiting for the next disaster to happen, and then beg Moses once again to save them as usual.

After what was a long meeting, they unanimously agreed upon the elimination of all the Children of Israel and Moses himself as well. All of them would be killed instead of being allowed to depart out of the country safely, as Moses had asked before. Accordingly, the leaders and chiefs of all cities had to prepare urgent plans to execute that mission, starting with the bringing together of soldiers from all over the cities.

After the meeting, Hori angrily returned to his work headquarters, where he informed his assistants about the recommendations from that meeting. He asked them both to prepare their own preliminary plans, to be submitted to him swiftly. Then he left.

Up until the previous day, Hori had only been feeling his way slowly towards the truth, but after that meeting, things began to change. He saw the Pharaoh as a leader of the whole country, but in a weak position. Also, he wondered how a magician could threaten a superpower country at that time, especially if its ruler was a god: Pharaoh. The Pharaoh's anger, loud voice, and threats to kill all the Children of Israel were not signs of his power, but they were strong evidence of his severe weakness. At that moment, Hori became quite sure that the Pharaoh was not a god. If he had truly been a god, he would not be shaken by the so-called magic of Moses. He became quite sure, too, that Moses was not a magician, and that the power he wielded was not magic, but a supernatural power that came only from the true God. And God had warned them several times to believe, but they had not.

Hori burst into tears. Because finally he did believe in God.

He wept bitterly, thinking he was far too late to help anyone. He cried for all the victims of that tyrant Pharaoh; and then he remembered Asmaya, and how her future would be. Eventually he decided to send Asmaya to Rachel, and to carry out a plan of his own—not the Pharaoh's plan.

At that time, prophet Moses was inspired by the Lord to leave Egypt by night with all the Children of Israel, as there was a plot to pursue them all. So they all prepared themselves, and waited for the appointed time.

Rachel thought of Samatya and Hori. She was quite sure that they did love each other and were suffering, but both of them had acted out of egotism. Besides, Hori had to know that his wife would soon be leaving Egypt with them all. So Rachel sent Benjamin secretly to Hori to inform him about the matter.

The next morning, Benjamin headed to Hori's mansion, hid himself a short distance away, and waited for him. No sooner had he spotted Hori's waggon going out of the mansion than he rushed towards him. The guards immediately prevented him from getting close to Hori, but Hori ordered them to let him go, and to return to their places.

"Good morning, sir. I've got a message for you," Benjamin said.

"What is it?" Hori said.

Benjamin looked at the driver, and stayed quiet, Hori realised that Benjamin didn't want the driver to hear what he was about to say, so he got off the waggon and pulled Benjamin aside: then Benjamin passed on to him Rachel's message.

Hori thought quietly for a moment, then whispered to Benjamin, "Listen, Benjamin, rent a waggon and wait for me by the outskirts of the city at noon. Stay there and don't so much as move until I come to you. Do you hear me?"

Benjamin nodded yes to him.

"Now go," Hori said.

Benjamin went quickly, while Hori walked slowly back to the waggon until he was quite sure that Benjamin had left and nobody could follow him. Then he beckoned to the driver to move off.

On his way to work, he thought deeply about how to carry out his plan, while time passed quickly, and all the Children of Israel would be leaving the country the following evening. Eventually he decided to stay in the city as long as he could, and then would follow them at the right time.

He arrived at work headquarters, and held a meeting with Horemheb and Akhnu. After he had heard their preliminary plans, he then started to explain his own plan to them.

"In the first place, it is vitally important to secure each city internally with enough soldiers before the mobilisation process for the attack on the Children of Israel.

"On the other hand, the western borders must be completely secured with enough troops as well, to counter a potential external attack. This is, of course, the mission of the army troops. So, the mobilisation process must be executed gradually and wisely without prejudice to the internal security.

"This should not take less than two weeks, otherwise we

will lose tight control over the lands, and there could be the potential for chaos. Anyhow, the Children of Israel won't slip out of our grasp." Thus Hori suggested at least two weeks so that he could delay the planned attack by the Pharaoh's soldiers on the Children of Israel for as long as he could.

The meeting continued for a long time, then Hori said, "I've got to go out briefly. I'll be back soon. Both of you carry on till I return."

No sooner had Akhnu gone back to his room than one of his spy soldiers came rushing in to see him, and told him that a man from the Children of Israel had passed on a message to Hori earlier that morning, but Hori's driver couldn't hear what the message was. Akhnu wondered what could be going on between Hori and the man in question, and was furious that they couldn't hear the message.

"Listen, you fool," Akhnu said to the spy soldier. "Hori's about to go out now. You follow him, and don't you lose him even for the blink of an eye. And don't ever let him feel that you are watching him, otherwise I will cut your head off. Now get lost."

After a while, Hori left the building, and headed to his mansion, driving his waggon himself. As soon as he arrived there he informed the chief housekeeper that he would take Asmaya to her mother's relatives for a few days. Additionally, he told her that she had to bring painters to renew Asmaya's room, engrave her name and her mother's name on the wall as well, and to finish the job as soon as possible. Hori then went out with Asmaya, and headed to where Benjamin was waiting for him.

He talked to Benjamin for a while, then gave him Asmaya, and waited till the waggon had melted away into the crowds, with Benjamin and Asmaya heading for the Children of Israel's village. Then he returned to work.

The spy had already returned to Akhnu and told him all that had happened. Akhnu was highly delighted. Eventually he would manage to corner Hori, and then it would be easy to get rid of him swiftly.

"From now on you are not a fool any more," Akhnu joked with the spy soldier. "I will promote you to the position of chief of fools." Then he laughed out loud, and made his way immediately to the Pharaoh's palace.

After quite some time, Benjamin arrived at Rachel's house without incident. He handed Asmaya over, along with some parcels of gold, and said, "Hori sends his regards to you, mother, and glad tidings as well. He is now a believer, and will follow us soon, but will try to hinder the Pharaoh's soldiers as much as he can as they are planning to attack us all. And he entrusted you with Asmaya."

Rachel was surprised. She had never expected that her prayers would come true so fast. She shed tears of joy and said, "Thanks be to the Lord."

Samatya was inside, and she heard everything that Benjamin had said. She couldn't believe her ears. She was smiling and crying at the same time. She had only tasted such happiness once before: fifteen years ago, when she declared her faith to Rachel. Eventually she became reassured that whatever happened later on, she would finally be together with Hori in Heaven. She rushed out of the room and said, "I heard everything, mother, I forgive him for everything." Then she took Asmaya from Rachel softly, and hugged her tenderly.

Meanwhile, Akhnu arrived at the Pharaoh's palace, and asked permission to see him urgently. The Pharaoh was still in the meeting with his senior counsellors. He was somewhat mystified by Akhnu's request, especially as he had never met him before, but he permitted him to enter. He beckoned to Akhnu to wait outside after he had heard what Akhnu had to tell him.

"What do you think?" the Pharaoh asked his counsellors.

The chief architect said, "My holy lord, for myself I trust Hori. He was accused before, and then he proved that he was innocent. Also, I think that man who is waiting outside is plotting against Hori. As you know well, my holy lord, you assigned Hori as a successor to Nakht, while that man was one of his close assistants, and of course he would have expected to take over Nakht's position."

Then, the Pharaoh looked over to Haman, as he wanted to hear his opinion. Haman kept silent for a moment, as if he was thinking about what the chief architect had said. Then he spoke.

"I suggest—and it is for you to command, my holy lord—that we put Hori under severe probation for a time, to find out what he is planning," he said. "Then surely we will know whether he is innocent or not. As for sending his daughter with a man of the Children of Israel to wheresoever, it won't be of much importance to us as we will kill them all soon or later."

All other counsellors agreed with Haman's point of view. Then the Pharaoh summoned Akhnu, and ordered him to get back to his work immediately and never to speak to anybody about that matter.

The same day, after Hori had returned to work, he discussed once again with Horemheb and Akhnu the details of the plan, and asked them not to go back home before they had finished the draft of that plan so that he could submit it himself the following morning to Haman.

Akhnu got very confused during that meeting, and said to himself, "There is something wrong here. How would Hori put together this tight plan to eliminate the Children of Israel while he was sending his daughter to be with one of them? Did the soldier lie to me? Or what exactly is Hori planning? I don't understand any of it."

Meanwhile, at the Pharaoh's palace they were still in the meeting. One of the spies entered and informed them that Hori was also holding a meeting at that moment with Horemheb and Akhnu, and that Hori would submit his plan to Haman the next morning.

"I told you—I trust him," the chief architect said.

The Pharaoh noticed that Haman was quite quiet and thinking deeply about something, so he asked him, "What is the matter, Haman?"

"My holy lord," Haman said, "I think that either Hori is plotting something very big against us, or Akhnu is a liar. At the same time, the records of Hori that I have don't indicate that he would dare to plot against us. I was also told that he'd asked his chief housekeeper to bring some painters for the renewal of his daughter's room. So we have to keep an eye on him day and night."

The Pharaoh laughed, pointed to Haman's head, and said to his counsellors, "I told you many times, this man's mind is not easy."

Then all of them burst out laughing.

Hori returned to his mansion, and asked the chief housekeeper how the redecoration of Asmaya's room was progressing. She told him that the workers had started already, and would come the next day to carry on. He went with her to the room to check, gave her some other instructions, and told her that they had to finish that work soon.

At the same time, what Hori had said to the chief housekeeper was reported to the Pharaoh's palace immediately.

Hori went to his room and stayed awake till the next morning. Then, he went to work as normal, picked up the draft of the plan, headed to the Pharaoh's palace, and met with Haman. He explained his plan in brief to Haman, who praised it and told Hori that his and all other leaders' plans would be submitted to the Pharaoh that same day.

Then Haman asked him about his daughter. Hori smiled quietly, and replied confidently, "She is alright, sir. I try as much as I can to compensate for the absence of her mother, and now her room is being prepared as befits the granddaughter of Sir Nakht."

Haman smiled at him whilst still somewhat bewildered.

Hori left, profoundly worried by Haman's question about Asmaya. He felt that he had to hurry and catch up with them in the village of the Children of Israel.

The hours passed slowly until the sun was about to set. He left his mansion and headed to his old house, followed by four spies. He entered the place, and changed his clothes to disguise himself as an old man, as he used to. Then he stood for a while in front of the house, in the garden, watching Samatya's plant. It had become a lush garden full of palms and tall trees whose branches and twigs went everywhere, and even overhung the fence and the street.

Then he went out, disguised, on his horse. The spy soldiers were quite sure that it was Hori, as he had entered the house alone, and it was now empty. One of them rushed back to inform Akhnu, while the other three followed Hori.

Hori had sensed that he was being followed, so he tried to elude them, but couldn't. Then he ran faster, but they were about to catch up with him. Suddenly, he turned round, and fought with them. After a prolonged struggle, he managed to kill two of them, while the third one ran away back to Akhnu.

At the same time, one of the Pharaoh's spies dashed into the hall at the palace, bowed to the Pharaoh during his meeting with his counsellors and said, "My holy lord, I have just received fresh news that all the Children of Israel are about to leave Egypt tonight. Also, we got further news from Akhnu that Hori ran away in disguise."

At once the whole palace was shaken by the Pharaoh's loud shouts. He immediately issued a royal decree that all available soldiers who were already assembled must be mobilised at once, and he himself would lead them. And Moses and all the Children of Israel were to be killed even if they had already left the country.

He turned to the chief architect and shouted angrily, "Is that the same Hori whom you trusted? He plotted against all of us; and when I get back, I will check for myself whether you helped him or not." He gave orders for Hori to be killed, and for Akhnu to take over his position immediately.

Akhnu received the news from the Pharaoh's palace. Finally, the moment for which he had waited for so long had come. He gave instructions to Horemheb to be ready with the soldiers till he came back, as he wanted to have the honour of killing Hori himself. On his way, Akhnu met with the third soldier—the one who had run away—and told him what had happened. They ran quickly in order to catch up with Hori.

Immediately, Horemheb decided to run after Akhnu, to

save Hori, and to depart with the Children of Israel as well. At that time, the sun had already gone down, and it was time for all the Children of Israel to start moving.

Hori rode fast, as if he was flying through the air on his horse, in order to catch up with them before they left. After him was Akhnu and the soldier, in order to kill him, and after them all was Horemheb, to save Hori.

At long last Hori arrived in the village, but no one was there; all of them had already left. He felt fairly reassured that they *had* left, and continued on his way after them.

A good while later, all of them were drawing level and could see each other: Horemheb, Akhnu and the soldier, and Hori. Horemheb cried out loud to alert Hori. Hori didn't hear him but the soldier did, so he turned back to Horemheb and fought with him. Horemheb killed him at once. Then, he also continued on his way after Akhnu and Hori, and kept crying out loud to alert Hori once again. No sooner had Hori heard Horemheb's shouts than Akhnu's treacherous spear struck him between the shoulders. He fell from his horse, and down to the ground.

After Akhnu had fulfilled his dirty mission, he turned back to Horemheb. They drew their swords, and fought each other long and hard; a long fight between good and evil that night, a night that was about to end. At last, Akhnu's head rolled on the ground till it finally stopped close to Hori's feet, with its frozen-open eyes staring at Hori's sandals.

Horemheb rushed towards Hori, to find that he had passed away already. He hugged him and wept hard. After that, he buried Hori quickly, then remounted his horse; and taking Hori's horse with him as well, he set off again to catch up with the Children of Israel.

He finally got closer to the host of the Children of Israel to the extent that the back group of the host were listening out for the sound of horses' footsteps behind them. Horemheb cried out loud and said, "Peace be upon you all. Don't be scared. I believe in the Lord of Moses and I'm coming with you. The Pharaoh and his soldiers are on their way now. Hurry up; move faster." Then he got off his horse, and threw his sword before them on the ground as a peace sign.

All of them marched towards the Red Sea, and Horemheb walked amongst them as well, his eyes deeply saddened, leading behind him the two horses on which some children were riding; while Samatya carried Asmaya and walked together with Rachel; and next to them Benjamin with his wife and children. All were silent and exhausted.

Then the news spread quickly amongst them about an Egyptian knight who had joined them at the rear of the host. Samatya got excited and said to Rachel cheerfully, "Hori came and joined us, mother."

Rachel smiled at her and said, "Yes, daughter, he has been true to his covenant with the Lord."

No sooner had Samatya felt that Hori had joined them than her enthusiasm was much increased, and she spurred Rachel into moving faster as Rachel seemed to be very exhausted. And she kept looking behind her every now and then, as she was expecting Hori to come.

That night walked slower, dragging its black cloak on the ground, while they all kept moving faster despite their severe fatigue. Eventually, the sun threw out its rays with which it spun a new dawn in front of them, while the earth disclosed an ugly face to them when they spotted, far away but within sight, the Pharaoh and a huge host of his soldiers heading towards them amidst a sandstorm. Suddenly, the sound of screams and shouts of panic from women, children, and even men, rose up into the sky. They were all quite sure that they would be overtaken either by the Pharaoh's soldiers or would be drowned in the sea.

Samatya kept screaming, crying and calling Hori, but she couldn't even hear her own screams among the noise of the others'. Rachel closed her eyes and kept praying.

Moses (PBUH) said to them all, "Nay, verily with me is my Lord. He will guide me."[3] Then, he was inspired by the Lord to strike the sea with his staff.

All at once the sea was parted, the waters on each side piling up and towering over them, becoming like a huge, firm range of mountains, the roar literally drowning out the noise of screaming and shouting, They turned and looked towards the roaring sound, and were surprised to see a dry path for them in the seabed. They all rushed forward and crossed all together, their shouts of terror turning into shouts of joy and happiness that they had finally been saved.

Samatya could not believe her eyes. It was the second time her eyes had seen a miracle within fifteen years. She wished then that she could see Hori, to share with him such moments, but she was quite sure that he had seen that miracle too, and that he was looking for her among the crowd as well.

All of them crossed peacefully and safely to the other side.

Then Moses tried to strike the sea again but he was inspired by the Lord: "And leave the sea as it is. Verily, they are a host to be drowned."[4]

Then, the walls of water collapsed and fell back in so that

---

[3] Holy Qur'an, Chapter 26, verse 62.
[4] Holy Qur'an, Chapter 44, verse 23.

the Pharaoh and his soldiers were completely overwhelmed, and drowned. And then the sea became flat and calm.

Samatya's eyes didn't stop looking among the crowds for Hori, but uselessly.

"What a good smell!" Rachel said.

"It is the smell of the sea, mother," Samatya said.

"No, daughter, it is not," Rachel said.

Samatya smiled and said, "It is the smell of freedom then, mother."

Suddenly, Rachel fell down; she couldn't move any further. Samatya knelt down beside her, and tried to help her to stand up again, but Rachel didn't respond to her at all; and she was staring up towards the sky.

As Samatya cried out, calling her, Benjamin and his wife rushed towards them; but Rachel had already passed away. Samatya burst into tears on Rachel's chest, hugging her with one arm, and carrying Asmaya with the other one.

And only then Samatya realised that the good smell that Rachel had sensed was nothing but wafting breezes that had just descended from the high Heavens a while ago.